NIGHT FALL

A GIA SANTELLA CRIME THRILLER
BOOK 7

KRISTI BELCAMINO

LIQUID MIND PUBLISHING

Liquid Mind Publishing
This is a work of fiction. All characters, names, places and events are the product of the author's imagination or used fictitiously.

GIA SANTELLA CRIME THRILLER SERIES

Enjoying the Gia Santella series? Scan below to order more books today!

Vendetta

Vigilante

Vengeance

Black Widow

Day of the Dead

Border Line

Night Fall

Stone Cold

Cold as Death

Cold Blooded

Dark Shadows

Dark Vengeance

Dark Justice

Deadly Justice

Deadly Lies

PROLOGUE

THE CASTRO, SAN FRANCISCO

He slipped into the club through the alley door.

The throbbing music vibrated through his body, adding to the nervous tension already flowing through his limbs. He made his way down a dark hallway that smelled like stale beer and sex, keeping his eyes trained on the flashing lights coming from the main room.

He stepped inside the cavernous warehouse filled with sweaty, writhing bodies swaying to the heavy beat. Disco lights overhead gave flashes of body parts. A sliver of a white smile. A shimmer of a sequined blouse. A slice of red-painted lips.

He paused in the doorway to gain his bearings. Then he turned so his back was to the masses and quickly checked his phone. The find-your-phone app he'd hacked into and modified revealed his target was across the dance floor against the far wall.

The area to his right harbored a bar where bored bartenders might remember his face. To his left was where the DJ and his two cronies had set up their gear. Both areas flanking the dance floor were well lit—the brightest spots in the club. He doubted anybody would give him a second glance, but just in case, he would take the most direct route—straight across the crowded dance floor.

He knew he was justifying his actions. He knew that what he really wanted was the electric spark from brushing up against so many bodies. A crowded dance floor was an excuse to have his flesh pressed up against someone else's—someone who would never allow that to happen in any other situation.

It had been a long time since he'd had to pay for that kind of skin-on-skin contact—after all now he had a regular girl who wanted it as badly as he did—but that didn't mean he took it for granted.

The anticipation of what he was about to do also filled him with a special energy—a burst of adrenaline and endorphins that made him feel invincible. The smell of perfume and deodorant mingling with body odor, the flashing lights and bodies undulating, and the bone-rumbling beat of the deafening music seeped into every fiber of his being. It was intoxicating and made him feel electric.

He wove through the mass of unwashed bodies, inhaling deeply as he brushed by each one. He had nearly reached the edge of the dance floor when he spotted his target. A mop of curly black hair blended into the dark wall behind the young man. The target's head was bent down over a bright phone screen, fingers tapping away.

Keeping his eye on the target, he stepped clear of dance floor and made his way to the wall. The target didn't notice him. Soon, he was standing directly beside the young man, who didn't look up from the screen or seem to register the new presence beside him.

Without looking directly at the target, he scanned the people nearby including the dance floor crowd a few feet away. Nobody was watching. Nobody cared.

Inside his deep coat pocket, his fingers clenched and unclenched around the knife's smooth handle. He was about to take the knife out when a woman approached from the dance floor.

Her hair was damp around her face from dancing, small tendrils sticking to her temple. She wore a black strip of fabric as a skirt and a tight, red tee-crop top that hugged her curves and revealed a tight and tanned abdomen. Her eyes were huge orbs and her lips full under a regal, Roman nose.

Two pairs of leopard-print sandals with stiletto heels dangled from her fingertips where she held them by their straps.

"Excuse me?" Her voice was nearly inaudible against the throbbing music. The young man didn't look up. She tried again, impatiently tossing her hair. "Hello? Excuse me?"

Her sleek thighs were inches away from him, but the target didn't notice her until she nudged him with her knee, her bare leg touching his thick jeans.

When the young man looked up, his eyes grew wide.

She said something else. He gave her a blank look. She leaned down near his ear and shouted, "Can I put my sandals under your chair while I dance?"

She didn't wait for an answer. She tucked the sandals under his seat, straightened, and was gone. The young man stared after her for a second and then dipped his head back down to the phone.

The man clutched the knife again, relieved that his were the sort of looks that rendered him nearly invisible to women like that. He'd been less than a foot away, and she'd never even given him a glance. If she had, her gaze wouldn't have lingered on him. He didn't mind. It was his super power.

It was how he was able to do what he did so well.

And now it was time for him to implement that art, to employ his expertise.

He leaned over slightly and jabbed the knife into the back of the target's neck in one smooth gesture and then yanked it back out again swiftly, severing the spinal cord at the brain stem. The blade went in so deeply that his fingers on the handle touched skin. He gave one expert tug on the knife to extract it and then quickly stuck it back in his large pocket. The victim's head slumped forward. He pushed it back so it rested on the wall behind them.

It was a lethal technique that had taken him years to perfect.

It involved plunging the knife between the vertebrae, cutting through the disc to sever the spinal cord. The person didn't die instantaneously but would effectively seem dead, unable to move or speak for the few seconds they remained alive.

It took strength, along with skill. His daily regimen of pullups had served him well.

With hooded eyes, he surveyed the rest of the room. He didn't find a single pair of eyes that met his and nobody quickly looked away. Only now, after several successful kills in less public settings, was he confident that he could pull off this type of killing in such a public arena.

He stepped three feet forward onto the dance floor and became one with the writhing mass of sweaty humanity.

1

The sky to the east was just blushing pink when I drained the dregs from my coffee mug and stood, turning around as I stretched so I could also take in the view from my rooftop terrace.

To my right, the skyscrapers in downtown San Francisco no longer glowed in the dark, but were morphing into tall, gray monoliths slowly being swallowed by the fog bank rolling in. Behind me, a few miles away, lay the Pacific Ocean, stretching to what felt like infinity. Soon, the fog devoured even the sun. My rooftop perch was transformed into a shadowy, shrouded oasis.

In the silence of the morning, I went through my daily ritual. I counted my blessings, saying what I was grateful for out loud. Each day, I named at least five things. It rarely varied. The first three were the same every day: My boyfriend James. My dog Django. Rosalie.

I wasn't sure how to categorize Rosalie.

The seven-year-old who lived with us was a special blessing. But I never knew how to refer to her. When I introduced her to others, I simply said, "And this is Rosalie."

Nobody asked for clarification. And I wouldn't have given any. It was complicated.

What could I say? This child is the daughter of the most powerful cartel boss in the world? She lives with us because she has nobody else? I will kill anyone who tries to take her away from me?

My gratitude practice took a sharp detour today. Instead of focusing on my gratefulness, an unexpected wave of panic and fear overcame me. I knew one day her father would come and try to take her away from me. It was inevitable. For now, our secret was safe. He didn't know she was his child.

But I couldn't trust his greedy wife to keep my secret forever. I could only hope that when she decided to betray me, she'd try to blackmail me first. I would pay for her to keep my most precious secret—that Rosalie was the daughter of her drug lord husband.

Thinking of the cartel brought back not-so-distant memories of how Rosalie had come to me—as part of a package of violence and unimaginable atrocities. I tried to shake off the dark memories.

The thick fog brought a chill with it that was made worse by my thoughts. I was done on the rooftop today. I wanted to be downstairs, warm and cozy with the people I loved.

Django remained curled up on his plush cushion until I stepped out from under the pergola, the low-hanging grape vines brushing my temple.

When I moved toward the stairs, he stood and stretched. He yawned, his big pink tongue sticking out in the dark for a second.

"Come on, boy," I said, waiting by the door to the stairs.

Downstairs, the loft was quiet so at first I didn't notice James at the table. He sat so still, steam rising from his coffee mug.

"Hey, baby," I said. I glanced over at the door to Rosalie's room. The door was shut tight. Django sniffed at the bottom of it and then curled up in front of it. He would stay there until she woke. I gave James a meaningful glance. These times alone in the loft were precious and few, snippets caught usually early in the morning or late at night.

James set down his coffee.

"Let me guess," I said. "The hackers still haven't relinquished control of the city's computers?"

He touched the tip of his nose.

"This article says the 911 operators can't log their calls and that patrol officers had to go digging in the basement to find paper citations to issue," he said.

"How archaic," I said. "The chief must be ready to blow a gasket."

The chief was our shared enemy. He was a corrupt, evil, son-of-a-bitch who had ordered James shot by my boyfriend's police colleagues. He'd hoped James would die, but the bullets had paralyzed him instead.

"It gets worse," James said.

"For us or for him?"

"Oh, him. Definitely him. It looks like if the city pays up, he loses all the funding for his helicopter. He must be pissed."

The chief had somehow convinced the city council to fund an outrageously expensive helicopter with night vision and heat sensors that the police department would use to fly over the city and "get the bad guys." Everyone knew he was going to use the helicopter for personal use—probably to fly him to his Marin County home every Friday night where he apparently spent his weekends. Loser.

The council had been scheduled to vote to approve the helicopter funding at Monday's meeting—the same meeting where the city council was going to vote whether to give in to the hacker's demands.

The hackers were asking for 500 bitcoin—roughly 5 million dollars. The city was on the brink of agreeing.

Each day, the pressure for the council to give in to the hackers grew.

The city had to bring in SWAT teams to an emergency city council meeting the previous night after irate citizens started to riot. SWAT ushered the council members out a side door. But one of them still got hit in the head with a cantaloupe one of the protestors had thrown. It was funny because nobody had been seriously hurt. But there were also rumors that the hackers had threatened doxing—going public with the personal information, including home addresses, of all the city council members if they didn't agree to pay up. The city had until Monday to fork over the money.

"The chief is fucked," I said.

"You know you turn me on when you talk like that," James said.

I laughed. "I got more where that comes from."

It was so nice to laugh with him. He'd been uptight lately. Every attempt he'd made to prove the chief was corrupt had been shut down. The chief was protected up high by powerful people. His reach extended to those in power in Washington, D.C., but James wouldn't stop looking for the chink in the chief's armor so he could take him down.

I knew he wouldn't rest until it happened.

But it made life in the loft tense. One disappointment after another. I hated to admit it, but it had affected our relationship. He was growing bitter and angry, and it broke my heart. At the same time, it made me want to spend less and less time with him. Who wants to be around a crabby guy all the time?

We'd also had a minor falling out recently.

He'd been contacted by a specialist he'd seen about his legs. They'd put him in touch with a team of doctors in Munich doing some incredible things involving stem cell research. A man had actually regained the use of his legs. But two other men in the clinical trial had died.

They wanted James to move to Germany for two years and participate in the experimental procedures.

As soon as he said there was a risk of death, I had balked.

I said. "I don't think you should go. If it works, it will be approved and available to everyone soon enough. You don't need to be their guinea pig."

At the time, I'd just woken up and was making coffee. It was too early in the morning for me to have that conversation.

"Gia, if it's approved, it could cost thousands of dollars, and it could be ten years down the road. If I do it now, it's free and I'd gain ten years of mobility. I could surf again, ride my bike...so many things."

James had handed me the bag of coffee beans as I took out the grinder from the cupboard.

Without thinking, I said, "Money's not an issue. I'll pay. I don't care what it costs. You know I have the money."

I could tell by the look on his face it was the wrong thing to say. My wealth was a sore point between us. He hated that I had so much of it. It was stupid. Why did he even care?

I pressed down to grind the beans, hoping he wouldn't be angry. As soon as the whirring stopped he said. "It could give me back my legs." He gritted his teeth as he spoke.

"You'd be gone two years! Two years, James."

"I can check if there's a place nearby for you to stay. I know you can't stay at the hospital. I did ask about that. About family."

Hearing him call us *family* triggered something inside. I was suddenly desperate. I realized I would do anything to protect this family we had formed.

"Please..." *don't go.* Even if I didn't finish the sentence, my voice was thick with pleading. I would get on my hands and knees and beg. He couldn't leave us.

I'd never been so weak, so petty, so selfish. I knew at that moment, I was being the most selfish I'd ever been in my life. And I'd been plenty selfish over the years. And then I dug the blade of guilt even deeper. He'd turned away and wheeled his chair toward the dining room table.

"What about Rosalie?" I said.

He froze. His hands stopped on the wheelchair's wheels.

It was the cheapest fucking shot I'd ever taken in my life. I was not proud. But I was desperate to cling to James and my life with him and Rosalie. What he was talking about would destroy our lives.

He pivoted, changing direction and headed for the elevator. I could tell by the muscle throbbing in his jaw that he was pissed. I watched, desperate, but knew there was nothing I could say. I'd give him time to cool off.

I'd called my best friend, Dante, in Sausalito, to cry on his shoulder.

"I blew it," I said.

"Why are you up this early?" he said.

I told him what had happened. He was quiet for a few seconds and then said, "Gia. It's his decision."

"I know."

"You can't guilt someone into staying."

"I know."

"So?"

"So what? Do you want me to tell him to go? To basically say, 'Hey, it's been great, but have a nice life?' Because if he goes that's what's going to happen. Two years apart."

"Can you move there?"

"I don't think so. I mean, it sounds like he'd be inpatient at this clinic. So, what, we would upend our whole lives and move there to see him during visiting hours or something?"

Dante went quiet again for a moment before saying, "I'm sorry."

"Thanks."

We hung up shortly after that.

There was nothing else to say. It sucked.

When James returned later, it seemed like he'd been punched. All the excitement I'd seen earlier was gone. He looked defeated. I waited for him to speak. He stared at me for a long moment. "I told them no. At least not right now."

A knot of anxiety formed in the pit of my stomach. Not *right now*. That meant maybe someday.

We'd made up since then. Sort of. But it was still tense, so this morning's laughter was welcome.

"We've got about an hour before Rosalie gets up," I said. He got my drift and started heading my way. By the time he reached me, I'd stripped off my sports bra and tugged down my yoga pants. His mouth was on my skin, and I forgot everything else. Cartel leaders, bloodshed, and bodies hanging from trees were extinguished by the touch of the man I loved.

2

I'D JUST KISSED JAMES GOODBYE AS HE WAITED FOR THE ELEVATOR door to open when Rosalie padded out of her room in her nightgown.

Wiping the sleep from her eyes with the back of her hand, the whoosh of the elevator door opening sent Rosalie racing across the loft, her dark hair flying behind her. "James!" She wrapped her arms around him. "You know you can't leave without saying goodbye to me!"

He kissed the top of her head.

She drew back. "Right? You have to say goodbye, right?"

"Right," he said. "I was just seeing if you were paying attention."

She frowned. "You wouldn't really leave?"

The mood in the room had suddenly grown dark.

He reached for her hand. "No way." His voice was solemn.

I could see her shoulders relax and she nodded. She was fighting back tears. I crouched down beside her. "How's this? From now on, we won't even hit the button for the elevator until you say goodbye?"

She pressed her lips together tightly and nodded.

I hugged her. Over her head, I exchanged a look with James. He gave a small grimace.

Sometimes we forgot that even the smallest things felt like they had life-shattering potential to this girl who had been through more in her short life than a room full of crime victims.

After the elevator door closed on James, I headed toward the kitchen, saying over my shoulder, "What will it be today? Oatmeal? Pancakes? A smoothie?"

"Pancakes!" I could hear the smile in her voice.

I'd thrown that option in even though we usually only had pancakes on the weekend. I wanted to erase the sorrow that had seeped into the room.

Although I never pushed for details, I knew that in Rosalie's life there had been more than one instance where she'd been robbed of the ability to say goodbye to someone she cared about —*permanently.*

The fog had lifted by the time Rosalie and I stepped outside our building. Her school backpack was nearly as large as she was. She wore a ruffled pink dress with white high-top Converse, and she wore her black hair slicked back in a long ponytail. I was helpless with hair, but over the past few months, she'd learned to fix it herself. As she walked down the sidewalk to the corner, her ponytail bobbed as she bounced along. My heart filled with joy. She could not look more adorable. Django trotted along beside her, keeping close.

I scanned the streets and buildings around us. My gun was tucked in a holster at the small of my back. I'd grown slightly complacent over the past few weeks since school started. At first, when we walked to school, I'd held tightly to her hand, and my head had been on a swivel, constantly alert for danger. But then I began letting her and Django walk a few paces ahead of me. Django was a pit bull mix who could look—and act—fierce when he needed to. I knew he'd rip out the throat of anyone who tried to harm Rosalie.

I'd grown to enjoy the morning walk to school and looked forward to greeting the regulars we came across each day. It made me feel more a part of the neighborhood. I loved the Tenderloin like it was a living thing, which in a way it was.

This morning, there was a slight chill in the air, which was typical for an early autumn day. It would start to get warm and beautiful again next month, in October. Most people didn't know summer in San Francisco could be bitterly cold, which is why, all summer long, the streets were filled with tourists shivering in shorts and expensive sweatshirts bought from tourist shops. Fall in San Francisco was the most beautiful time of year, a well-kept secret.

The energy on the streets made me feel alive. It was the throngs of people hustling on their way to work, clutching briefcases and insulated lunch bags and travel mugs of steaming coffee. The Tenderloin had slowly grown from a poverty-stricken, crime-ridden den of thieves into a working-class neighborhood with affordable rents in a city with one of the highest costs of living in the United States. My neighbors were city workers, housecleaners, high-rise janitors, waiters, bus boys, sanitation workers, teachers, hair stylists, and so on—people who worked hard and deserved affordable rent in a safe neighborhood.

First there was Jimmy, the homeless guy who slept on the sidewalk in front of an apartment building on our block unless it was cold and then he reluctantly used the key I'd given him for a small, empty office space.

"Ms. Rosalie," he said, giving a small bow. "How are you this morning?"

"Fine, Jimmy. And you?"

"Living the dream. Living the dream."

It was strange to think about, but he was telling the truth. Jimmy was an Iraq war veteran, and hell for him was anyplace with four walls. He said he felt trapped and claustrophobic unless he was sleeping under the stars. I'd tried to talk him into a place down the street where he could sneak up to the roof and sling a hammock and sleep every night, but he said he felt trapped staying in one place. I didn't point out that he slept in front of the same apartment complex every night. But maybe he needed to be on the move like he said, because if you went by his spot during the day, he'd cleared out. He only returned at dusk.

Before we walked on, Jimmy slipped Django a treat. I don't know where he got them or how he could afford to buy dog treats when he seemed to barely have enough money for food, but every weekday morning, he had something for Django. Needless to say, my dog loved him and wriggled excitedly as soon as Jimmy appeared on the sidewalk in front of us each day.

"Do we have time to see Darling this morning?" Rosalie asked.

We often stopped into Darling's salon if we were early where I refilled my travel mug with her fancy coffee before we continued toward the school. Darling had the busiest hair salon in the city, but she made her big money in providing false papers. She specialized in fake IDs for women trying to escape domestic abuse.

"Not today. She's out in the East Bay this morning." I knew because I was meeting her there later.

Rosalie pouted.

"But," I continued, "Danny's going to watch you after school today, so that should be fun."

When Rosalie first came to stay with me, I'd drop her off at Darling's salon. All the stylists would keep an eye on her as she sat and did homework or drew in her sketch pad.

But recently I'd asked Danny, my young hacker friend, to watch her. He was teaching her computer skills and showing her how to fly his drones. Even though he was embarrassed, I insisted on paying him for child care.

Part of the reason I'd connected him with Rosalie was because I knew he was lonely. He wouldn't admit it, but sometimes me or James were the only visitors he'd have for months at a time. He said he had friends, but I knew they were "online" friends.

I worried about him a lot. I'd only recently learned he had a disease that made him grow too much and would cause him to die young. It broke my heart. I tried not to think about it too much, or I'd lie in bed and cry.

He seemed to really like Rosalie. The two of them each had some deep, dark shit in their past to deal with, and I think they recognized fellow spirits.

"Danny? Super!" Rosalie said. She skipped ahead with Django at her side. She'd wasted no time learning American slang by watching TV. Her English had been pretty good before she came to live with us. Now, you'd never know it was her second language. She was a smart little girl.

I watched her ponytail bounce as she and Django trotted ahead.

The San Francisco streets were already busy as we approached one of the main arteries, Market Street. Horns honking, the hydraulics on buses, and the screech of the light rail combined with the chatter of pedestrians in suits talking on their cell phones and the distant wail of sirens.

Rosalie, who was about twenty feet in front of me, came to an abrupt halt at the crosswalk for Market Street even though the sign indicated she could walk. She looked back to see if I'd noticed. I smiled. I'd warned her about crazy San Francisco drivers and told her, until she was older, she should always wait for me to cross even though her school was directly across the street and some of her friends were already out on the sidewalk.

The first thing I noticed was that the sirens had grown much, much louder. At the same time, a vehicle rounded the corner two streets down from us. It was racing through traffic, going up on the curb and sidewalk to avoid slower cars, sending pedestrians screaming as they hurled themselves out of the way. In the distance, at least five squad cars with lights and sirens blaring were barreling our way—pursuing the car. The vehicle, a beat-up American sedan, swerved and was headed toward Rosalie and Django. My heart leaped to my throat. I ran toward them even though I knew there was no way I could reach them in time to push them out of the way.

At the last second, the sedan slammed into a light post a few feet from Rosalie. It wrapped itself around the pole in a thundering crash of shattering glass and twisting metal.

I was at Rosalie's side then. She stood wide-eyed and staring, only ten feet away from the destruction. The police cars had all caught up, coming to a skidding stop in a semi-circle in front of us. The driver didn't look good. He was slumped forward on the steering wheel. Shaking, I quickly stepped in front of Rosalie and took her hand. Django was glued to her side, whining softly.

I heard screaming and saw a crowd gathered around someone on the ground. The sedan must've hit at least one person. Quickly, I ushered Rosalie across the street. Traffic had stopped. I shielded her as we walked. She tried to glance back, but I slowed so my body was in her way. Neither of us spoke until we were inside the lobby of the school. She tried to look behind me at the wreck again, but I turned her body so her back was to the door. I crouched down before her. "Are you okay?" I asked softly.

She nodded, but she was biting her lower lip. I could tell she was holding back tears.

I thought it best not to mention what a close call it had been. I wasn't even sure if she realized the car was headed directly her way.

"Are you going to be okay to go to school?"

With all the trauma Rosalie had suffered in her life, I didn't force things. If she needed a mental health day, she got it. She was seven. It wasn't like she was going to miss some crucial piece of information for Christ's sake.

"Yes. I'm fine."

My little stoic.

At the door to the school, I leaned down before her.

"Danny is going to pick you up from school today, remember? You can call me if you need anything. Anything? Okay?"

She nodded.

I'd given her a little flip phone so she could always call me if she needed anything. Frankly, it was more for me than her. She'd never used it. But I didn't know if I could leave her at school or anywhere else without her being able to reach me. She'd been taken away from us once before.

I hugged her. "Okay, then. Bye."

She began to walk away and then turned back to me, her forehead scrunching up.

"Is he dead?"

Her eyes looked past me at the wreck across the street. A firetruck had pulled up, blocking our view.

I swallowed. I'd promised to always be honest with this little person who had seen death firsthand and witnessed rapes and atrocities that most people never see in a lifetime.

"He might be," I said.

She nodded. Standing there in her pink frilly dress and high-top tennis shoes, she made the sign of the cross—not the Italian way but the Mexican way, kissing her fingertips at the end.

I tried to hide the look of surprise on my face. She turned and walked up the stairs to the school before I could say a word.

Outside, with Django at my side and waiting for the light to turn so I could cross, I dialed James and told him what happened.

"Jesus Christ."

"I know," I said. Then I told him about Rosalie making the sign of the cross. "Do you think we should take her to church or something?"

My mother had been Catholic, and I knew her faith had meant a lot to her. I'd lost my faith when everyone in my family had been murdered.

"Maybe you should ask her," James said.

"Good idea."

Sometimes that man made too much sense.

"Listen, I gotta go. That's my other line," he said.

James now worked as a private detective after the chief had not only fired him from the police department but also went after him with bullets.

He took on some cases to keep busy, but his main focus was nailing the police chief. We'd come close last year, but the higher ups protecting him had stepped in. We hadn't given up. In fact, Darling had lured me to the East Bay by promising she might have information that would help us go after the chief. I couldn't wait to find out what it was.

But I also felt a wave of sadness that James had hung up on me so quickly. It used to be we'd talk for hours about nothing. Lately, he was always in a hurry to either get out the door or hang up.

I tried to brush off the disappointment. I didn't know what demons he fought. He'd lost his beloved career and the use of his legs in one fell swoop.

The light changed, and I was able to cross the street, giving the accident site a wide berth. Even though I didn't want to look, I did. I watched as they maneuvered the driver's body out of the crunched car's window. His head flopped forward. Even though I didn't see blood or other injuries, I knew. Dead as dirt.

Without thinking, I made the sign of the cross and kept walking.

3

Twin Peaks, San Francisco

"Hey, baby."

Blake opened his eyes, squinting against the bright beam of sunlight streaking in through his window and illuminating the red sheets on his bed.

The girl next to him lightly ran her fingers down his bare chest.

He took her hand and sucked on her fingers one at a time until she climbed on top of him.

He made sure she orgasmed before letting himself go.

She was sweet. A nice girl. But he was wary of letting anyone get too close to him. He had too much to lose. Even though it was Sunday, he was going to have to blow her off.

"Blake?" Her brow furrowed. "Everything okay?"

"Sorry," he said, kissing her cheek. "Listen, I've got a busy day today. Let's grab some breakfast, and I'll drop you off at home before I get to work."

They dressed and stepped outside of his room. His roommate Kraig was slumped over a massive bowl of cereal. He wore a ratty plaid bathrobe, and his hair stuck up in all directions. He was an at-home day trader, so he rarely had to actually get dressed. But he did have to get up in the middle of the night to work the overseas markets.

"Jodi," he mumbled.

"Kraig," she said with a smile and then reached for Blake's hand. She was so damn sweet. He wished he could fall for her. But he was still in love with his ex. It was a disaster.

After breakfast, Blake kissed Jodi goodbye outside her apartment door.

She sighed and stretched. "I feel like the luckiest and unluckiest girl at the same time. Both."

He smiled. "Why's that?"

"Did you see all the women checking you out at Café Stella? And you were with me. You didn't even look away from me for two seconds. You're something else, Blake. You're honest. You don't even swear. I've never heard you use a bad word. You're the type of guy every woman wants to bring home to their mother. But I'm so unlucky."

His smile grew wider. "Why?"

"Because your work is more important than me," she said and frowned. "What do you do all day on your laptop anyway?"

"I told you baby, I'm a day trader."

"You can work at home?"

"Yep. That's the beauty of it."

"But it's the weekend," she said, pouting.

Leaning over, he kissed her mouth. "I've got admin stuff to do. See you tomorrow night? Dinner?"

"Fine!" She pretended to be mad but couldn't pull it off and burst into laughter.

He waited until she was safely inside before he got back into his Lexus and drove to the San Francisco Library. There had been a text from his right-hand man.

MagnusOpus was the only one who had this number. Blake had reluctantly provided it after one of their biggest clients had gone missing along with some of the bitcoin he'd owed another client. Eventually they found out that the client had been arrested and therefore couldn't provide the drugs he'd been paid for, nor return the money.

The customers on Blake's dark market website, Night Fall, all had complete anonymity, so after that fiasco, he'd posted a disclaimer that he couldn't vouch for the trustworthiness of anyone using the site and that people used the site at their own risk. What the heck were they going to do anyway? Go to the cops? To report their own illegal activity on an illegal website? Whatever.

All his employees had strict orders to communicate only by way of the encrypted employee chat room he'd set up on his dark web site to maintain security. This had better be good.

As he strode into another coffee shop near his apartment, Blake found the first free table where he could keep his back to the wall so nobody could see his laptop screen. He quickly logged into the chat room with his username, VladTheImpaler.

"What's up?"

"Dude. I think I found out where that missing bitcoin went."

MagnusOpus was really his old friend from high school, Carl—one of the few people in the online world he trusted.

Blake sat up. About 500 bitcoin had gone missing from his escrow account the day before. That was more than $5 million. MagnusOpus had been working furiously nonstop to trace the path of the withdrawal.

"Talk to me."

"I traced the bitcoin leak to an IP address in Iceland."

"Oh yeah," Blake took a sip of his espresso.

"I don't know if you know this, but when Storm quit yesterday morning, I was able to gain brief access to her computer for a time."

"Why?"

"I wanted to make sure she wasn't taking any of our secrets with her, you know. I didn't see anything weird. All she had were some travel documents. She's since deleted them, by the way. She's supposed to fly to Iceland tomorrow morning."

"Who the heck is she in real life?" Blake asked.

"I thought you might ask that," MagnusOpus said. "She's local. Her name is Charlie Koleman, 1644 Athens Street, San Francisco."

Although the website promised complete anonymity, Blake insisted MagnusOpus keep a file with the real names and identities of all Night Fall's employees.

Blake sat back when he saw the Bernal Heights address. They were practically neighbors. She lived less than four miles away.

MagnusOpus typed more. "What do you want to do about her?"

Blake paused. He had been so careful about who he hired to work for his website. Night Fall had a reputation to uphold. In two years, his little love project had exploded, and now he was pulling down more than a billion in sales a year. He didn't have time for little traitors to jeopardize his operation.

"You need to get a message to her telling her if she doesn't make a deposit of bitcoin equaling $5 million in the next 24 hours, she's dead."

The screen was blank for a few seconds. Feeling as if he needed to argue his case, Blake typed more.

"She could take us down. We could lose everything."

He waited...thirty seconds, sixty seconds, staring at the blinking cursor waiting for a response. Would Carl be on board or not?

"Good plan. That will send a message to anyone else who thinks they can fuck with us."

4

I walked further south on Market Street until I spotted the gateway to Chinatown. I'd worn my workout gear under my trench coat so I could fit in a quick Budo session before heading over to the East Bay to meet Darling.

Darling had texted me the night before saying she had heard that the police chief was meeting with some FBI agent in an undisclosed Oakland location. The agent was flying in from the east coast this morning. She'd heard the clandestine meeting was about the hackers who had taken over the city, but she wasn't sure.

I asked for the federal agent's flight info so I could tail him from the airport to the meeting. From what Darling had told me, the agent might not be on the up-and-up. If I was lucky, I could see—and hopefully take pictures of—the chief meeting with the agent. Because there had to be some reason the meeting was secret. The chief was surely up to no good.

My mind was on all this as I walked into the dojo, apparently scowling.

"Gia *san*? What's wrong?" Kato tilted his head, a concerned look on his face.

"Sorry," I said. "I was thinking about our police chief. And it was pissing me off." I purposely didn't mention the close call with the fleeing driver and Rosalie. It made me sick to think about it.

"That would make anyone upset," Kato said. "You can direct all that disgust toward the kicks you are throwing my way. Got it?"

I dropped my trench coat onto the floor and kicked off my shoes. "Let's do this."

Ninety minutes later, I stepped out of the dojo feeling like a million bucks.

Years before, after I'd been raped and lost my parents to murder, I dealt with my problems by drinking too much, doing drugs, and sleeping with anyone that had a pulse. I probably would've kept sinking until I was a homeless addict, but for some reason, I'd had the survival instinct to beg Kato to take me on as a student.

Budo had saved my life. I often worked out at home, but there was nothing like having Kato push me to the extreme. He was not only my sensei; he was my friend. He could read me the instant I walked into the dojo and sense what kind of workout I needed.

Within the hour, I was on the back of my Honda Blackbird motorcycle. I'd showered and changed into black jeans, a black leather moto jacket, and boots. Once I was on the Bay Bridge I rode the white line, zipping in and out of traffic. It gave me the same thrill I used to get racing my Ferrari up and down the coast. Nowadays, I no longer had a death wish, so I didn't do anything stupid. But I still managed to get the adrenaline rush I so desperately craved. No badass workout at the dojo could stifle that urge.

The drive to the airport was smooth, and I pulled up to the fence near where the private jets landed. Right on time, I saw the jet dip down and glide toward the waiting livery car. I had a lot of questions about why an FBI agent flew on a private jet and had a car waiting for him. A lot of questions.

I watched with my mini binoculars until I saw the guy get into the back of the car. I started the bike and headed toward the road where I could easily drop in behind the black town car and tail it to its destination.

Once we were on the freeway, I stayed about five cars back, sometimes more, so I wouldn't arouse suspicion. When the town car exited onto Lakeshore Boulevard in Oakland, I slowed and pulled to the shoulder. At that spot, the freeway was elevated, and I had a clear view of the exit. The town car turned right toward the lake and downtown. It took a wide curve and then another left. That led into the park area where the boat launch was.

Soon I was at the launch and spotted the car in the parking lot. I parked my bike out of sight around a corner and casually walked along the jogging path on my side of the street. I took out my phone and sat on a bench pretending to read something on my phone. My eyes, behind dark glasses, tracked the fed's every move as he got out of the car and paced the parking lot.

He had his cell phone pressed to his ear. He was so typical. He wore a dark, three-piece suit. He had close-cut hair and was as nondescript as they come. Total fed.

A few cars drove by. At one point, the fed stopped dead in his pacing. His back was to me. He then slowly turned, holding the phone at his side, and stared directly at me. I held my breath. He'd spotted me somehow. He lifted his hand in a lazy wave at the same time my phone buzzed.

Before I could react, he was back in the car and speeding

away out of the parking lot. By the time I raced over and got on my bike, the car had disappeared. My phone buzzed again. I looked down at the text.

It was from Darling.

"You've been made."

5

HUNTER'S POINT

It seemed darker and more ominous in this part of San Francisco.

His fingers clenched and unclenched into fists on the sleek leather seat. He could almost feel the blade in his hand again.

The Cleaner gave the man beside him the side-eye as he'd slipped into the backseat of the car. It looked like some government car. He didn't get it. But whatever. The guy was paying him good money.

The man beside him didn't even look when the Cleaner sat down and slammed the car door behind him. The man looked like a drill instructor. Went by the username The Patriot.

How plebian, the Cleaner thought.

The Patriot had found him through Night Fall—a darkweb market where he'd posted his resume, so to speak. The client, whoever they were, had agreed to the Cleaner's terms—to deliver the cash to him in person. The Patriot was the middleman. Because while every other idiot on the website dealt in bitcoin, the Cleaner refused to do so—at least for the first job he did for someone. He didn't play by anyone else's rules. He *made* the motherfucking rules.

He thumbed through the thick envelope of cash that had been waiting for him on the seat of the car—American dollars, just as he'd specified.

It was a different gig than working for the Hong Kong crime lords. They were classy. They wore designer suits and jewelry, and when they did meet him in person they summoned him to back rooms in luxury hotels and restaurants.

But they also didn't pay nearly as well.

The man sitting next to him stared straight ahead as the car wove through the Hunter's Point neighborhood. It was a stupid meeting place. Cops everywhere. If the Patriot had been smart, he'd have asked to meet in Russian Hill or someplace the cops ignored because all the fucking rich people never broke the law. He laughed to himself.

But no, this jerkoff had wanted to meet in the most dangerous neighborhood in San Francisco that was crawling with cop cars. What the fuck? It'd been a pain in the ass to get down here. It wasn't as bad as it used to be—back in the day, city buses had to have police escorts, according to the Uber driver who dropped him off there. But it still was a place where murders happened more often than not. Or at least that's what people said. After a year here, he still considered himself new to the city, so he didn't know for sure.

What he did know was that it was going to be bitch to get back to his house. And he'd have to contend with whatever fuck-wads tried to mess with him on the streets while he waited for his expensive Uber ride to show up. Apparently, there was a fucking surcharge to drive to this area. Of course there was.

He could handle anyone who tried to mess with him—even a group of wannabes. It was easy to take out the first few. And most of the time, any of the other so-called tough guys would fucking hightail it out of there after the first one fell. But what a needless bother. And, after all, nowadays he liked to be paid for murder. It felt like a rip off to kill someone without getting paid.

He gave The Patriot another glance. The guy hadn't looked over at him once. He could shove his knife right through the man's thick neck and slice his jugular so easily. It would take seconds and then he'd open the car door and be gone.

The Patriot finally turned to look at him, focusing black eyes on him that didn't blink. There were few things in the world that made The Cleaner uneasy, but this guy's stare did.

"Okay." The Patriot said. It wasn't a question.

The Cleaner nodded.

They came up to a red light. There was a group of thugs on the corner. The car stopped right beside them. One of the guys, wearing low slung jeans and a bandanna wrapped around his head, started to step into the street toward the car.

Inside the car, he tightened his fingers on the knife that lay on the seat beside his thigh.

The look he gave the thug must've worked because the thug gave a slight nod, turned his back on the car, and began to walk in the opposite direction. The others followed suit with only one guy turning to give the car a last glance.

The dickhead beside him cleared his throat again. "There's more where that came from," he said. "You're going to be busy. I'll be in touch."

Without answering, The Cleaner tugged on the door handle. He hopped out and slammed the door behind him.

6

THREE WEEKS BEFORE

Blake examined himself in the mirror. He wondered what women saw in him. He knew he attracted female attention everywhere he went, but he wasn't sure why.

He'd been told he looked like the guy who played the vampire in *Twilight and* some guy from a 1980s show, *Beverly Hills 90210*. He didn't see it. But he still had appropriated the username Vlad, in a nod to the vampire character. Everyone on Night Fall knew him as VladTheImpaler.

He liked designer clothes, but he wore them easily and sloppily, buying thousand dollar shirts and then leaving them untucked or even wearing them with stains.

But today he wanted to look good.

Melissa, his ex-girlfriend from back home, had texted that she was in town on business. Surprise!

"Ethan, I can't wait to see you. I've made reservations at Epicure for lunch."

He'd meet her at the restaurant. He couldn't take the chance that his roommate would find out that Blake wasn't his real name.

An hour before they were supposed to meet, he showered and dressed carefully. Melissa had expensive taste and had always liked it when he wore designer clothing. He decided to wear Louis Vuitton worn-look jeans, Gucci polished shoes, and a black Dior silk shirt that he left unbuttoned a little. He put on his heaviest gold necklace, a 24K gold bracelet, and some cologne. He looked in the elevator mirror on his way out. Not bad.

He bought a dozen red roses and arrived early, so he was waiting at the table when Melissa walked in. He stood and hugged her. She looked like a freaking million bucks. He was half hard just from hugging her. She had on a tasteful white dress that clung to every curve. It was silky white and, with her platinum blonde hair catching the overhead light, she glowed like an angel. She somehow managed to look both sexy and innocent at the same time.

After they had finished a bottle of wine, she leaned over, her eyes soft and lips glistening. "Why didn't we work out, baby? We could power a goddamn skyscraper with the electricity between us."

He smiled. It was better not to speak. He was prepared when her smile disappeared and she drew back. "Oh, yeah. How dull. Because you decided your calling in life was to deal drugs online."

"I told you I don't run that website anymore, Melissa."

"Really?" She tilted her head. He could tell she wanted to believe him but didn't. "Even having you as an *ex*-boyfriend could hurt my career. If you were still my boyfriend, it would all be over."

"Then you could be a housewife," he said, joking.

She glared at him.

Melissa was the lieutenant governor for the state of Virginia.

She'd run for office on the governor's ticket, and the governor had made his mark by being outspoken against drugs. During the election last fall, Blake had paid $500,00 to a turd journalist who had threatened to expose the relationship between him and Melissa.

Blake had been devastated when she dumped him telling him that his thriving business would ruin her life. He'd lied and told her he'd sold the website, but she didn't believe him. He moved to San Francisco partly because it hurt too darn much to see her beautiful face on every billboard in town during the race. And he'd hoped to somehow get over her with some physical distance between them.

But then she does something like this—comes to town and calls him.

"I'm sorry, baby," she said, reaching over and squeezing his hand. "In another lifetime, we would've been married by now with two little kids and living in the suburbs. You'd be a salesman and I *would* be a housewife."

She burst into laughter. She was drunk. "Okay, maybe not a housewife."

"Hey, there's nothing wrong with being a housewife," he said, half serious. His mother was the strongest and smartest woman he'd ever known, and she'd spent his childhood working at home.

"That's why I wish you'd never started that website, Ethan."

It was weird to hear his real name again. He'd gotten used to Blake.

She sat back and looked sad. He didn't know what to say, so he didn't say anything.

"The governor is going to retire," she said with a loud sigh. "He wants me to run in his stead. He is ready to endorse me, but he said I needed to get married. If I want the female vote, I need to be a married lady with kids. How stupid is that, right? He said I'm less threatening that way, and more women will relate to me."

"What are you trying to say, Melissa," he said. He could feel his heart race. Was she here to tell him she was getting married?

"That comment about nothing wrong with being a house-wife. The way you helped that elderly woman across the street earlier. I saw. Right before you walked in here. I was paying my driver. I saw it. Or how about the way you've donated to missing children's organizations since you were in college?"

"What's your point, Melissa?" He smiled. The wine was starting to make him feel warm and fuzzy.

She leaned forward. He was suddenly mesmerized by her lower lip as she spoke. He was suddenly tempted to lean over and kiss her mouth.

"My point is, Ethan, you'd have made a hell of a governor's husband."

She sat back. The spell was broken.

He swallowed. "I still could."

She shook her head. "Ethan, let's get real. You started the world's largest online drug dealing site. Even if—and that's a big if—you haven't been involved with it in a year, you're still a stain on any political career. I'm sorry. I do still love you, you know. And you know what sucks? You never used to lie. You used to be the most honest man I knew. Running this website has made you a liar. I'm sorry."

Her voice was cold and filled with disdain.

He pushed back his chair. "You're not, actually. Sorry that is." His voice was low and tinged with sadness. "Let's just face facts. Your thirst for power is greater than your love for me."

He wasn't angry, just incredibly disappointed and weary. She looked at him with hard, cold eyes without a trace of warmth or sympathy. He shook his head and stood. He set five one hundred dollar bills on the table and said, "Dinner's on me."

He took one last look at her, and walked out.

7

I PUNCHED IN DARLING'S NUMBER.

"What the fuckity fuck?" I was still staring in the direction the federal agent's car had taken, even though it was long gone.

""Mmmhhhmm," she said. "This is bigger than I thought."

"Why do you say that?" I knew I'd been too obvious and scared him off, but I didn't know what she meant. "And how the hell did you know he'd spotted me?"

"We got a line on his cell phone. He was talking to the police chief. Somehow they knew about you and told him. I tried to warn you. Did it work?"

"Your text came at the exact moment he turned around and stared me down. He took off out of here pretty fast. I don't think I can catch up, even if I'd left immediately. Want me to at least try?" I had one leg already slung over my bike.

"No. I think we'll let this one go."

I was disappointed.

"I'm going to text you an address. I want you to meet some people."

"I'm on my way."

———

IT ONLY TOOK me fifteen minutes to find the house in Berkeley. It was on a shady street lined with trees. It was a typical hippie area with bright-colored Victorians in ramshackle shape. Party lights hung from trees and porches. Funky sculptures, wildflowers, and prairie grass took over front yards instead of manicured lawns. The blue and purple Victorian was set quite some ways back from the street.

Darling had told me to pull down the long driveway and then park behind the house where my bike wouldn't be spotted from the road. She said the back door would be unlocked. I was to enter and then wait for instructions. It sounded like James Bond stuff, which made me snicker. Darling could kick James Bond's ass. Well, maybe not because he could probably just shoot her, but she was a force in her own right. If you took weapons out of the equation, she could take him. She was a big woman but moved like a panther. After she pounded Bond, she would probably charm him with her big Cleopatra eyes. They'd be friends by the end.

I stepped through the back door. I was in a small, closet-sized space. No windows. A panel on the wall that looked like a speaker and a steel door leading into the house. A holding room.

"Gia!" Darling's voice startled me. It came from the panel on the wall.

I hit a button to respond. "What now, boss lady?"

"Marcus is going to come down and search you. I hope you aren't carrying."

"Fuck yeah, I'm carrying." I released the talk button. I was instantly annoyed. Someone was going to search me? No way. I punched the talk button again. "I'm not giving up my gun. If they don't trust me based on your word, then fuck them."

Darling gave a long sigh. "Stand by."

After a few seconds, she said, "Fine. Good Lordie, you are so difficult." She mumbled the last few words, and I grinned.

About five minutes later, the steel door clicked and swung inwards.

A man with dreadlocks stood in the shadowy interior. He was not smiling. I decided two could play at that game and walked in, brushing by him. Beyond him was an empty room save for a set of stairs. I was tromping up them when I heard the steel door slam behind me.

At the top of the stairs was another steel door. I leaned against the wall, waiting for the dreadlocked guy to get there and let me in since I didn't see another speaker box.

He took his sweet time and gave me a slight eye roll when he saw me leaning against the door. I smiled and winked at him. He made a slight sound to indicate his exasperation with me. Whatever. Wasn't the first time someone reacted to me that way.

This time, he strode right into the open doorway before I could move. He didn't wait to see if I followed. The door opened up into a massive room. The entire space, which was basically the top floor of the house, was filled with desks and flickering computer screens.

Hackers.

I'd always imagined a hacker den to be a dark, shadowy space lit by flickering computer monitors, but this place looked like a goddamn operating room. Everything was gleaming silver and white. The sterility of the room was tarnished by the motley crew of hackers. One or two looked like the computer nerds they were, but the rest ranged from the dreadlocked reggae-looking guy to the sorority-type girl with a blonde ponytail, pink sweatshirt, and fluffy bunny slippers propped up on her desk.

I spotted Darling over in the corner. She was ensconced in a white leather chair. Her lioness mane of dark curls bobbed as she nodded hello to me.

Next to her, in a black leather chair, was a man who looked like a young Steve Jobs, even down to the black turtleneck, loose jeans, and wire-rimmed glasses.

I headed her way.

She smiled.

"Hey, baby girl," she said. "This is how we go after the chief, Gia," she said, throwing her arm out to indicate the worker bees around us.

"I like it." I said.

"This is just the East Bay crew. Most hackers work alone. But Marcus and Isaac set this up as sort of a co-op space. For the more social hackers in PeopleUnited."

"PeopleUnited?" I said.

"That's what we call our loose coalition," the turtlenecked man beside her said and smiled at me. "I'm Isaac."

"Isaac. Gia." Darling said to introduce us. "You've met Marcus."

We both nodded.

"What's the plan?"

"Follow me," Isaac said.

The three of us followed him into another room.

"Hold up. I got questions," I said, holding my palm up.

"Yeah, yeah, we're the ones holding the city hostage, yada yada," Isaac said.

"Okay, good," I said and turned my attention to the monitor. "Do you think that's what this meeting between the chief and the FBI agent is about?"

"Probably," Isaac said.

I didn't like that answer.

"We'll explain over brunch," Darling said. "I'm starved."

8

HE'D CLEANED HIS APARTMENT TWICE THAT DAY. BUT THERE STILL seemed to be dust settling on the wooden desk pushed up against the window. He opened the top drawer in the kitchen, pulled on a new pair of white gloves, and retrieved a microfiber cloth out of the package.

Twenty minutes later, he threw the gloves and cloth in the trash can and surveyed his work. No dust on anything. Then he scowled. In a beam of light streaming through the window, he noticed more dust motes swirling. He felt the anger and frustration rising from his core—a crimson mass that was writhing and spinning inside him, traveling up to his throat, seeping into his mind, making his face feel hot so that he thought he might actually be seeing red.

He clenched his fists and closed his eyes. He waited but the fury didn't subside, so he allowed himself a small pleasure—he retrieved his latest kill to the forefront of his mind so he could savor the memory.

Standing upright, eyes closed and fists clenched, he walked himself through the dark nightclub, his mind's eye focused on the target. As he remembered, the smells and the sounds and the view came back sharply, and his body began to relax. He unclenched his fists. But his eyes remained closed as he remembered taking the knife and plunging it into the young man's neck. As he remembered this, his entire body jolted in pleasure, and his eyes snapped open.

Killing was his only release.

And in between kills—a period which usually lasted months, if not years—he parceled out moments where he could appease his need by remembering. He often only allowed himself these moments of immersive memory when his need was so great he feared killing someone without forethought and planning. He knew doing so would be the end. Unplanned violence and death would result in him being caught. Methodical planning and caution meant he could continue.

But The Patriot had given him the greatest gift—a series of killings that were all supposed to take place within a few week's span. He would have these fragments of memories to draw on for months of dry spells.

He glanced at his watch.

Twenty-four hours until the next one.

And seven of those hours he'd be sleeping.

He could wait.

It would be worth it.

Midnight, his hairless cat, had come out from under the bed and was curling herself around his legs. That's when he knew it would be okay. The cat sensed when he was in the danger zone and hid. But she also sensed when he'd returned to the loving owner who pet her and fed her and let her sleep curled up around his head on the pillow each night.

A surge of guilt soared through him as he looked down at the sweet little face looking up at him.

He leaned down and scooped her up, holding her up to his face and nuzzling her so their noses touched.

"Who is my baby kitty?" he said. "Who is the best cat on the planet? You are. You don't have to be scared of me. I promise. Don't worry, Daddy would never, ever hurt you."

9

THE CAFÉ ON TELEGRAPH AVENUE HAD A BACK ROOM. IF YOU parked on the side street, you could access it through a door in the alley.

These were Darling's specific instructions to the two men in the Berkeley Victorian—go in through the alley door.

As soon as I walked into the back room, Darling patted the chair beside her.

"I'm starved," she said, giving me a doleful look with her massive black eyes. "I can't think until I eat."

Inside the back room, Darling ordered a pot of coffee and four full breakfasts: eggs, bacon, ham, hash browns, and toast. The works.

The waiter, a rail-thin kid in tight skinny jeans and a white Replacements T-shirt nodded, his long bangs flopping.

Marcus and Isaac arrived at the same time as the food. Nobody spoke until Darling had tucked into her eggs and ham. After a few bites, she looked up and smiled.

"Okay. My brain is functioning again. Marcus, would you mind filling Gia in."

The guy with dreads put down his fork. The air grew still.

"Do you know what hacktivism is?"

I didn't like the way he stared at me, waiting.

"Activist hackers," I said nonchalantly with the implied "*duh!*" right there. I scooped a bit of egg with my fork and put it on a small bite of toast.

"How familiar are you with what they do exactly?"

Time for bluffing was up.

"Not very," I said and shoveled the egg bite in my mouth. "I mean you obviously are trying to take the city's money. Is there some altruistic purpose to this besides just ripping them off?"

Isaac's eyes widened. "Well, *yeah.*"

I raised an eyebrow.

"We're taking that money so the chief doesn't get his helicopter funded."

"Brilliant," I said.

"Are you being sarcastic?" Marcus said. "If the chief's helicopter gets funded, the money comes directly from the funding set aside for homeless youth. That means more kids on the streets doing drugs. More addicts. More violence. More cycle of abuse. Would you like to hear more? Do you think that's brilliant?" He was smug and patronizing. I hated him.

"Fuck you," I said, staring him down.

He frowned at Darling. "I don't have time for amateurs—or smartasses."

"And...I don't have time for pretentious assholes." I slammed my mug down, spilling coffee and scooted back my chair. I stood and turned toward the door. Darling gave me a wide-eyed look, but before she could speak, the dreadlocked man gave a loud sigh.

"Please sit," he said, gritting out the words. "I'm sorry."

"Marcus doesn't mean to be a dick, he's just too smart for us average plebes, which means he isn't always capable of social graces," Isaac said.

My blood was boiling, but I sat back down.

"I'm here for Darling only. If she says I should listen to you, you have ten minutes." I picked up a fork and gestured at my plate. "Or until this is gone, whichever comes first."

As I continued to shove my breakfast into my mouth, I didn't take my eyes off Marcus as he explained. My stare didn't even faze him. Sociopath.

He finished speaking before I was done chewing my last bite of toast.

The gist of it was that his group, PeopleUnited, was part of a larger, loosely organized hacktivist group in the Bay Area that worked to stop powerful people taking advantage of the little guy. Always through hacking. Sometimes that meant prying into the personal information of a restaurant manager sexually harassing his employees. Sometimes that meant digging into the personal accounts of citizens who were abusing their children. And sometimes it meant seeing what the local politicians were up to in their spare time.

"Got it," I said. "How does this concern me? Am I just here because Darling told you I have a hard-on for the chief?"

The guy named Isaac flinched. Whatever. I didn't have time for prima donnas.

"We've got a problem," Marcus said. "While we are very interested in the chief's relationship with the FBI and are intent on shutting down the funding for his helicopter. Something else had cropped up that is even more pressing."

I waited.

He continued. "There is a website on the dark web called Night Fall. It's basically a market place. We think the chief has some connection to it. It started out as a safe place for drug dealers and buyers to exchange product. But it's grown into something dangerous. It's a place to buy and sell just about anything."

"Like what?" I asked.

"It's grown to include the sales of weapons including assault rifles—I'm talking in bulk. Which of course any terrorist could jump on. But that's not the worst of it. It's recently become a way for people to hire hit men and now, possibly even worse."

"No shit, huh?" I said.

Darling nodded, pressing her lips tightly together. "Mmmmhmmm."

I sat back, thinking about that.

"But that's not why we care," Isaac said.

I sat back up.

"Recently, one of our members also happened to be employed by Night Fall," he said. "She left because in the employee chat room, the founder—who goes by VladTheImpaler—said he'd okayed a few posts that involved selling young women. He apparently put his foot down on child trafficking but said if the women were at least eighteen, he'd approve the posts."

Marcus nodded. "Exactly. So, our girl, Storm, wanted out. She left. But somebody didn't like her leaving. They arranged it to look like she also took some $5 million dollars worth of bitcoin."

I raised an eyebrow.

"They threatened her. Gave her 24 hours to return the money. But she didn't have it. She came to us for help."

"Does she have the money?"

"No. And she told them that, but they don't believe her," Isaac said. "She came to us for help three weeks ago. Five of our members here in the Bay Area got upset on her behalf. Really mad. They formed a vigilante group with Storm. Call themselves the Omega Six. They were able to hack into Night Fall, which isn't some small feat.

"The Omega Six messaged the site founder, goes by Vlad-

TheImpaler, and told him they'd hacked into Night Fall and copied many of his internal documents. They warned that if he didn't back off Storm, they'd dox him—expose a file that contained thousands of his customer's IP addresses and identifying information. It would be devastating to the website, which operates on the premise of anonymity. It could shut the whole thing down."

At this point I was riveted. I realized I'd been holding my fork in the air for the past few minutes, frozen. I set it down and waited to hear more.

"How do I play into this?"

"Instead of backing off Storm, they took a different tack," Isaac said, shooting a meaningful glance at Marcus.

"They are killing off the Omega Six. One by one," Marcus said.

10

TWO WEEKS BEFORE

Melissa had him rattled.

Didn't she know he'd started Night Fall so she would respect him? So she would want to be his wife? All his hopes and plans and dreams had shattered when she dumped him. Everything had gone sideways except one thing—Night Fall had grown to be wildly successful, bringing in more money than he'd imagined in his wildest fantasies.

It both thrilled and terrified him.

Instead, his success had meant he lost the woman of his dreams.

But right now he had bigger problems.

He'd set up the website to make it impenetrable, yet somehow, the Omega Six had hacked into the system. He stayed up all night examining the code, trying to figure out where the backdoor was, where they had snuck in. He had Carl working on it full time as well. As much as he hated to admit it, he wasn't as surprised as he should've been that someone had hacked in. When he came up with the idea of Night Fall, he'd taught himself how to code. He'd never considered himself an expert at it, and now he was paying the price.

He didn't know that when he went after Storm, she would have a small army of hackers backing her. But he could handle it. Carl was working on finding the identities of the six. The beauty of making millions of dollars a week running a site like Night Fall is that you could buy anything under the sun on that site with that money. And that included buying hacker expertise. He would fight fire with fire. He would learn the real names of the Omega Six and kill them one by one.

Then, yesterday, an article on Night Fall had been published by *BitGeek Magazine*, mentioning that the site was now a forum for people to hire hit men. Crap. The U.S. Department of Justice was holding a press conference that morning about Night Fall.

This was not the kind of publicity he'd hoped for. Even so, it'd helped business. The article had spurred a wave of new users who decided it would be pretty darn cool to buy some ecstasy or Vicodin online. The article—the second the tech magazine had run on him—once again used the nickname they had coined for Night Fall: the Home Shopping Channel for drugs.

So, while business was booming, he was worried about the feds closing in. Carl had come across a new user who seemed suspicious—a guy going by the name of HardKore. Carl had traced the guy's IP address to Washington, D.C. An FBI office. *Holy smokes.* Not cool.

Blake had immediately reached out to the police chief, who'd told him not to worry. His FBI contact was taking care of it. That's why he paid the chief the big bucks.

Kraig knocked on the door. Blake opened it wide.

"Hey, there's a piece of mail here for an Ethan, but it has your last name on it. Is that like a relative or something," Kraig said.

"Oh, yeah," Blake said, hoping he wasn't blushing. "That's my middle name. Weird."

He grabbed his jacket and headed out, snatching the envelope out of Kraig's hand as he passed. He glanced down. The envelope didn't have a return address.

It was postmarked San Francisco.

It was only when he was safely seated at a table down the road in the Farallon Branch of the San Francisco Library that he opened the envelope. His hands were shaking as he tore it open. A small key slipped out.

At first he didn't realize what he was looking at—then he remembered. It was from the police chief. The Patriot. Apparently, the hitman required cash. Not bitcoin. It would be a pain in the ass, but it was doable. He would go to the bank later today. The key was to the storage locker at the train station where he had been instructed to leave the cash.

He logged onto the private chat room in Night Fall. Carl was already online. "I've got the names of two of them. The Patriot is ready to rock and roll if you submit payment."

"Tell him it will be there this afternoon. For double the fun. And clean as a clear river please."

It was code. He was paying to murder two Omega Six members. He would pay extra for a "clean hit"—a nonsuspicious death. In this case, ones that looked like drownings not murders. The chief had said a clean hit would be easier for him to overlook, to cover up, to write off as an accident. Perfect.

He smiled. This stuff was fun. He couldn't wait until they found the real names of the other four members. It would be a good lesson as the business moved forward and grew even larger. He would make sure some people circulated rumors that the Omega Six had threatened him and ended up dead.

11

"Three of the Omega Six have died over the past two weeks," Isaac said and took a sip of his coffee.

"How?" I asked.

"Drowned."

"Wait? All three? You're kidding me?" I said.

"They're making it look like they aren't connected, but we know they are," Darling said. "Scott died first, drowned at Ocean Beach. Apparently, we're supposed to believe he took a midnight swim. In his jeans."

I frowned.

"Leanne drowned in her bathtub. They said she'd had too much to drink and took some OxyContin." Marcus said this, scowling and then muttered. "Kid didn't touch drugs."

"And Cameron drowned in his apartment pool," Isaac said.

"Did the coroner's rule all the deaths accidental?" I asked.

"There was no coroner's investigation. Open and shut cases. Cops said accidental death within moments of arriving on the scene. Police didn't even put up crime scene tape," Darling said. "Nothing. Cameron's mother asked for an autopsy but was told she'd have to pay for a private one. When she went to collect her boy's body at the morgue, he'd been 'accidentally' cremated already."

The chief. That fucker. And the hits were the work of a pro. They were clean. Not so clean that the victims simply disappeared but clean enough that they weren't suspicious.

All three stared at me wordlessly.

"How do they even know who you guys are? Who the Omega Six are?" I said. "Doesn't much of your strength lie in your ability to remain anonymous?"

The two men exchanged looks.

"We're trying to figure that out," Isaac said and met my eyes.

"We're assembling a team," Marcus interrupted. "Darling said you might help us if it meant bringing down the chief. We think he's the one paying the hitman. The remaining three members of the Omega Six, including Storm, uh, I mean Charlie, live in San Francisco. We need to warn them. We think that the Night Fall guys might have hacked our chat room. As soon as we figured out what was happening we reached out to the other three and told them to go dark. They did, but they don't know why. We didn't have a chance to tell them. We don't trust anything online. We might be dealing with hackers even better than we are. Ones who can remotely access every single thing we do online. We have to assume that their computers and our websites have all been compromised."

Isaac pushed over a sheet of paper. "If you want to help. We could really use it. Here are their real names and street addresses."

"In other words, you need me to communicate the old-fashioned way? In person?" I gave a wry grin. "I got you."

"Honey, these men don't leave their little dark cave," Darling said. "It's a miracle they came out to eat with us. Everything they do is on a computer."

I nodded.

"Plus, we are keeping everything that has been said here today under wraps. There might be a mole. If we get someone in our own operation to warn them, we might actually be leading the killer to them," Marcus said. "We just don't know who to trust or not trust at this point."

Darling cleared her throat. "I immediately thought of you and James because of the chief," she said. "If we can connect him to these murders, we've got him. You in, baby doll?"

Get the chief? Now she was talking my love language.

"Damn right I'm in."

12

THE FIRST NAME AND ADDRESS ON THE LIST ISAAC AND MARCUS gave me was in Noe Valley—what we called the sunny side of town. It was south of downtown San Francisco, heading toward the airport.

The main drag had trendy restaurants but also had laundromats and funky hole-in-the-wall boutiques selling dried-out crow's feet, incense sticks, and black magic spells to punish the ex-boyfriend who slept around while he was still with you.

Sam Lee's place was in a nondescript, two-story brick building off the main drag. A turquoise Vespa scooter was parked on the sidewalk in front of the first-floor garage. A large window took up most of the second story overlooking the street. I crossed the road to see if I could get a glimpse inside the apartment. The only thing I could see were the tops of some palm fronds and the back of a couch.

I rang the doorbell.

"Yeah?" It was a girl's voice that came out of the speaker.

"Sam?" I said, realizing I didn't know if Sam was male or female.

"He's not here."

"When will he return?"

"Dunno," the girl said.

"Today?"

"Maybe. He's been gone since Tuesday, so I don't know. Maybe he's not coming back."

Alarm zinged through me.

"Do you know where he went?"

"We're roommates, not fuck buddies. I gotta go. I'm late for work."

"What about places he liked to hang out?"

When she answered, she sounded exasperated. "He liked to go to Club Fuck sometimes. And he usually had coffee at Midnight Espresso around the corner."

"Can you get him a message?"

But then I realized she'd hung up. A few seconds later I heard a door slam, and a girl with pink-streaked hair wearing a gray hoodie and scuffed white Converse came out the door. She side-eyed me and tried to brush past, but I yanked her back by her elbow.

"Ow! What the hell are you doing?"

"He couldn't have stayed the night at Club Fuck or the coffee shop Where would he disappear to for days at a time? Does he have a girl or something?"

I stood between her and the sidewalk.

She jerked her arm away from me and rubbed her elbow. "I don't know."

I glared at her.

"Besides," she said. "If he had anyone it would be a guy."

I took my palm and pushed her up against the wall of the building.

"I'm trying to be polite here, but you are making this very difficult. What I want to know is if you have any idea where he is or where he might have been."

She squirmed free. I backed up. She rubbed her elbow again, glaring at me.

"I said I don't know,'" she said, widening her eyes. "He's a weird one. He usually just stayed in his room. The only reason I know he isn't here is because rent was due on Friday, so I knocked on his door. It didn't look like his bed had been slept in, and he hasn't come back yet. Now, I'm stuck with the rent."

"Did he usually pay rent on time."

"Yeah. For the past two years, he's been a perfect roommate —weird, like I said, stayed in his room all the time, but it was like I lived alone and he paid half the rent, so I got no complaints."

I moved out of her way, letting her pass.

She strapped on a helmet with a unicorn's horn and then hopped on the Vespa and zoomed off down the road. It was only then that I noticed she had a furry tail attached to the back of her pants. And *she'd* called Sam weird. Obviously, we had different definitions of the word.

Across the street, I got on my Blackbird and took off in the same direction. A few blocks away I pulled into Midnight Espresso and asked the barrista about Sam. She knew him.

"He hasn't been in for a few days, now that you mention it. He's pretty much like clockwork. Same drink, same croissant. Every single day."

I thanked her and was about to head over to Club Fuck when I noticed there were computers set up. It was an Internet café. I logged on to the city newspaper's website.

The front page was full of the hacker takeover and how they were trying to stop the police chief's proposal for his helicopter. I kept scrolling and then turned to the local section. I was looking for a drowning. But I found it under "Crime & Police." A murder in the Mission district, believed to be gang related, and then a murder at a gay nightclub, Club Fuck. A stabbing.

I sat back. It was probably Sam. But it didn't fit. All the other hits were drownings. Why would the killer switch it up this time? This was not a clean hit that wouldn't be investigated. I read on.

The article said investigators would release the name of the man pending identification from the medical examiner's office.

I looked up the number for the medical examiner's office and punched it into my phone. At least this office wasn't under police control. At least I hoped it wasn't.

"This is Macy Townsend from the Chronicle. Are you releasing the identity of the man found at the club yet?"

"Stand by."

After a few seconds, the man came back on the line. "Sam Lee. DOB 09-24-1999. Noe Valley. The individual was found deceased in a building in the 800 block of West 6th. The cause of death is a stab wound and the manner of death is homicide. The homicide unit of the San Francisco police department is investigating."

Of course they are.

"Thanks." I hung up.

I dialed Darling.

"We just heard," she said.

I needed to go back to Lee's apartment and look for anything that might point to the killer. Maybe the killer had reached out to Sam online to meet at the club or something.

"I'm heading back to his place to see if I can find out more."

"Can you check on the other two first? Warn them?" Darling said. "They both need to go into hiding. Especially Charlie. You can tell her she can stay with me."

Even though I was only a few blocks away from Sam Lee's house, I knew she was right. Searching his room could wait.

The next address was for Charlie Koleman.

The small flat was in a beige building in a row of apartments in Bernal Heights.

The door to the apartment was behind a locked gate. I slipped in just as a man in coveralls came out. He held the door for me and I smiled.

A woman answered the door. Her brassy hair was pulled back in a ponytail, revealing dark roots. She wore a baggy tank top over a sports bra and khaki jeans, and she held a dishrag in her hand.

"Mrs. Koleman?"

"Yes?"

"Is Charlie here?"

She shook her head, her eyes narrowing.

"Can I speak to you for a moment?"

Her watery blue eyes took me in. She decided I wasn't a threat and nodded, her bare foot pushing open the screen door for me to enter. Inside, she led me over to a worn out, brown plaid sofa. I sat down and she took a spot across from me in a ripped leather chair, wiping her hands on her shorts. A small trickle of sweat rolled down her temple. She was nervous.

One wall held several school pictures of a pretty sandy blonde-haired girl with cat-eye glasses.

"Is that your daughter?"

She stared at me and then tilted her head, not answering. I'd said something wrong. She stood. "Listen I'm busy, and I told you Charlie's not here."

"I'm terribly sorry to bother you, but this is important. A friend of Charlie's sent me. Do you know where she his?"

"A friend?"

"Yes, someone who is worried about her. We believe she is in danger."

The woman sank back down into her chair. "Yes. I know."

My heart raced.

"If you could just tell me where she is or get a message to her..."

"I never approved of her calling herself that—I still call her Charlotte." The woman gave a wry grin. "She thought Charlotte was too girly. Maybe it is. I'm sort of old-fashioned. At least that's what she tells me. Teenagers." She rolled her eyes as if I had any idea what she meant. "She said something about it being dangerous to be here. She left a few weeks ago."

"When's the last time you heard from her?"

"Last night. She called from London." Then she made a face shaking her head. "Oh god. She told me not to tell anybody where she was going."

"Don't worry. I promise I won't tell a soul. Like I said, a friend sent me. To warn Charlie. But she must have already known she was in danger."

The woman looked at me suspiciously. "She said something about some people coming to ask for her. People who wanted to hurt her." The woman's eyes narrowed and she stood again.

This time I stood as well.

"Mrs. Koleman. I promise you I'm not one of those people she mentioned. She went into hiding, didn't she? And you know what? She was very smart to do so. There's some bad things going on, and leaving was the best thing for her to do. At least for a little while, while we figure this out."

"We?"

"There are some of us who are trying to stop those people she warned you about."

"Does all this have to do with her online stuff?"

I nodded. I didn't want to say anything more than that.

"If anyone else asks about Charlotte, you tell them she left and wouldn't tell you where she was going, okay?" I said. "And why don't you buy a disposable phone at the drug store and give her that number the next time she calls. Those phones can't be traced."

Her eyes widened. "But I have a land line. I haven't got a cell phone yet. You think they could listen in to my phone?"

I pressed my lips together. "Maybe. Just be careful. And if you talk to Charlotte again, tell her that a friend of Marcus's came by and told her to stay gone for a while. I'll be in touch with you again once it's safe for her to return."

The woman's face had grown pale. She swallowed. "Okay." Her voice was hoarse. The sun was setting behind her, obscuring her face in shadows, but I could tell she was about to cry.

"It's going to be okay," I said. It was a weak attempt at reassuring her—and maybe even wasn't the truth—but I had to try.

By the time I hopped on my Blackbird and headed toward the bay, dusk had fallen. In the gloaming, as I rode on stretches of road without streetlights making my way down to the water, I felt invisible dressed in black on my black bike with my huge black helmet. As I shot onto a straightaway, street lights cast the city in an orange glow. In front of me, the San Francisco skyline flickered to life as white squares of light dotted the buildings. I headed straight for the stadium with its bright lights shining, a beacon in the dark.

13

HE HAD TWO MORE ASSIGNMENTS ON HIS PLATE. THE PATRIOT HAD said to spread them out. Terrence, the young man, first. And then Storm. The main target.

Like the night club contract, The Patriot said neither of these hits had to be clean—because unlike the first three hits where he had been careful to make them seem like drownings, something had happened that made the murders more urgent.

The Patriot had said that now the clock was ticking and it was more important that they just get done...before Monday. It was Saturday. But the Patriot also said he should make them all look different so it didn't seem like there was any connection. He could do that.

He was a fucking pro. One of the best of the best.

The Patriot said to wait to make a move or even do recon until he sent word it was go time.

As Midnight curled into bed with him, wrapping herself on the pillow above his head, he closed his eyes and visualized how he would execute his two next missions. Terrence was first. He'd concentrate on him.

The first thing he tried to do was hack into the man's cell

phone so he could pinpoint his location at all times. But the phone number he'd been given by The Patriot was not in service. He searched for the IP address of the target. Same. Nothing. Like he'd disappeared. That could only mean one thing—the target had been warned and gone underground.

He'd have to show up at the street address. It was his last resort option, but in this case it was necessary. That guy would put up a fight. He also lived in a rough neighborhood. It would be difficult to sneak up on him. He could do it, but he knew there would be lots of eyes in the neighborhood if things got loud and ugly. He had to think this one through. Terrence was married with a kid. He could use that. He smiled to himself in the dark. Yes, he could definitely use that.

14

A FEW BLOCKS SOUTH OF THE STADIUM, I PULLED DOWN A LONG, dark street dotted with crumbling apartment buildings. Rusted and dented vehicles lined the road. Many windows were still dark, waiting for residents to return home on the bus from far away jobs.

It was one of the few areas surrounding the stadium that hadn't been gentrified. It was only a matter of time before all these working-class families had their homes threatened the same way my Tenderloin neighbors had. If it weren't for Darling, the developers would have forced everyone out a long time ago.

The last address was for a Terrence Hall. The note Marcus had given me showed the guy's user name was ShadowKing.

I pulled onto the street. Several young men dominated one street corner under a light, passing around a joint, a few gracefully swaying shoulders and hips to the beat throbbing from an open window of a car parked nearby. They all stopped to stare when I rounded the corner near them. I lifted my leather-gloved hand in a salute and passed, parking at the far end of the street, jumping up onto the curb to save a spot for a car but also to protect my bike from being knocked over.

At the other end of the block, the young men watched me for a second as I took off my helmet and shook out my long hair. I ignored them as I locked my helmet to my bike handles. When I looked again, two of them were heading my way.

I didn't like the way one of them was walking. He was cocky. He looked like he had something to prove. And even though he was using one hand to hitch up his baggy jeans as he walked, the other was tucked tight in his jacket pocket, holding the fabric close to his chest. A gun or knife. I sighed.

I didn't have time for this shit. I kept my gaze averted until they were both in front of me.

"Whatcha want?" the dangerous looking one said, eyes glinting in the streetlight.

"Doesn't concern you," I said.

His jaw clenched, and I watched his tongue touch his upper teeth. He shot a glance sideways at his buddy. I ignored him—he was a bigger guy who made sure he was behind his friend's shoulder. He wasn't looking for a fight.

But this douchebag was.

I waited, tensed and poised, my feet planted shoulder width apart, knees slightly bent, hands in fists clenched at my side. I kept my eyes straight ahead, but I was really paying attention to his feet and legs in my peripheral vision. They would determine how this all went down. When he took a step forward, I knew.

Wrong move, buddy. He was within range. Big mistake. But I waited.

Then, there it was. The weapon. A gun. A knife would be more dangerous with him this close. Maybe something that would even make me turn and run. A gun? He was too close to flash his gun around. I could knock it out of his hands. He was wielding it to scare me, to threaten me. He probably wasn't going to just shoot me. Not without a conversation where he could first attempt to exert his dominance. At least that's what I was counting on.

"You're a mouthy bitch," he said. "This is my crib. If I ask what you are doing, you better fucking answer me and with respect."

I didn't have time for conversation so I looked away for a second, turning my head to look at the door across the street where I was headed. He turned to follow my gaze, and by the time he turned back, I'd executed my move.

I brought my right hand up and over, doing a karate chop with my hand bladed that struck his wrist and sent the gun flying. At the same time, I lifted my left leg and stomped it right down on his ankle, sending him careening forward and off balance. As he tipped toward me, I grabbed his shoulders with both hands, slamming him down at the same time I lifted my right knee and smashed it into his nose. I'm sure the guys at the other end of the block could hear the sound of the cartilage crunching. When I looked up, his big buddy had turned and fled, but one dumbass from the other corner was running my way, shouting, holding a knife.

As the thug cowered on the sidewalk at my feet, I walked over and kicked the guy's gun so it went skittering under a parked car.

The guy with the knife was coming closer. When he was fifteen feet away, I stepped into the streetlight and pulled up my black sweater, revealing my Ruger. He drew up short. I waited, not moving until he put the knife away. I kept watch as he yanked his buddy up from the ground and helped him back to the car. Soon all four of them had piled into the vehicle, and it left. I waited until I could no longer hear the thumping of the bass before I crossed the street.

As soon as I stepped in front of the door, it swung open. A young black man with glasses and a goatee stood there.

"You here to see me?"

"You Terrence Hall?"

"Yep."

He glanced behind him. I heard a sound in the darkened room. It was a baby making a soft cry.

"Just a second," he said. He stepped back inside and closed the door. I waited. I heard voices and then, after a few seconds, he returned with a jacket and car keys.

"I'd say I'll drive, but I don't think you want to leave your bike here when Rodney and his buddies come back. And they'll be back. Follow me?"

"Sure," I said.

"My car's around the block."

For a second I wondered if he was lying. He didn't know who I was. Was he trying to ditch me? I didn't think so.

15

THE MESSAGE CAME IN THE DEAD OF NIGHT. THE TEXT WAS AN alert that he should check new messages on the Night Fall website.

He'd nearly slept right through the notification buzz. He jumped out of bed, flinging Midnight off the side. The cat squealed and scurried into the closet.

In the living room, he sat at his desk and logged onto his computer. Soon, he was on the website with the coded message. Only once he'd read it did he allow himself to relax, sinking back into the hard chair.

The Patriot had pulled the trigger on the new assignment. Go after the young man with the family. Glancing at the time, he realized his best move would be to get there right away so he could watch anybody leaving the house for work or school or whatever.

In his room, the closet door was cracked. He threw it all the way open so he could extract a fresh white shirt and pressed black slacks. As the door screeched open, Midnight, who cowered in the corner of the closet, hissed at him. He aimed a kick at her head, but missed, swearing, and immediately felt guilty. But what the fuck? His own cat had hissed at him. He tamped down his anger. No time for that now.

16

"What's the word from the Patriot?" Blake typed the words in the chat room the second he saw Carl log on. He was glad Carl couldn't see him or hear his voice. If he could, he'd know Blake was freaking out.

"Storm is still on the lam. The Cleaner's going to go have a little chat with her mother and convince her to tell us where Storm is hiding out."

"Nice," Blake typed. "What about the other one?"

"ShadowKing is going to be tough, even for a pro hitter.

"Why?" Blake wrote.

"Dude is street smart. He's also a former gangbanger. Not your typical nerdy hacker," Carl wrote.

Blake closed his eyes. Darn. This was not going how he'd planned.

"What's the play?" he finally wrote.

"Our hitter thinks we can get to ShadowKing by kidnapping his family. Maybe even convince him to give up Storm."

"The Cleaner does kidnappings?" Blake said.

"Sure," Carl typed. "Why not. He's done them for ransom

before. If no money, the kidnap victim dies. But this time, everyone dies anyway."

Blake frowned. "How much is this going to cost us?" he wrote.

"Dude, she took nearly a million dollars. You gonna let her get away with that? And besides that, you know as well as I do, that with what she knows, she could destroy us in a heartbeat."

"But she's never threatened that ..." Blake wrote.

"Dude, it's fucking implied. She took the money knowing that if we bitched about it, she could just go public with all our personal shit. That's why she joined up with those hackers. She fed them all the shit they needed to get in our business. You know it's true."

"I don't know." Blake wasn't sure why now he was hesitating. "How much have we paid this guy already?" Had to be way more than Storm had stolen from them.

"It's the principle, man," Carl wrote. "With what she knows about Night Fall...if she takes it the feds... You heard what the chief said the other day, his inside man said the FBI is snooping around. For all we know she is working with them already."

A small part of him wondered how he could so blithely agree to kidnap and murder, but he shoved that part of him deep down inside. This was freaking survival, man. He had to save his own skin.

"So what do you say, boss?" Carl's words appeared on the screen, startling Blake.

It was up to him, wasn't it? He was playing God. Who should die? Who should live? It was up to him. And right then he was feeling magnanimous. Four people were already dead from his orders. What were two more?

"Tell him to try the kidnap first. If ShadowKing doesn't comply by giving us Storm, The Cleaner can kill them all."

"Cool. So you're okay with us paying for three hits instead of one?" Carl wrote.

"Four."

"Right. Four. You're okay with that?"

"We're already balls to the wall, my friend," Blake wrote.

There was no room for error.

It was his life on the line now.

17

I waited on my bike until a gold Camry stopped in front of me and flashed its lights.

Terrence Hall led me down the Embarcadero to Mickey's Diner.

"I haven't been here in years," I said, taking off my helmet after we parked.

He was flicking his keys as we walked inside. Nervous habit?

We sat in the old trolley car and dug into grilled cheese sandwiches and French fries.

In the light, I had a better look at Terrence. He wore wire-rimmed glasses and had a neatly shaved head and trimmed goatee. His fingernails were immaculate. His button-down gray shirt was pressed. He looked like a Stanford student. No more than twenty-three, I'd guess. All I really knew about him was that he was a hacker and lived in one of the rougher parts of town. I wondered if he was the father of the baby I'd heard.

I was hungry so I didn't say anything at first besides some random comments about the Giants game the night before. I hadn't eaten since breakfast with Darling and crew.

I only knew the ballgame details because James had decided

to discuss it with me in-depth last night in bed. Good thing I loved that man so much. Baseball put me to sleep.

Plus, I was hoping Terrence would start talking about why I was there first. I wanted to see why he decided to meet with me so easily. Finally, after we both polished off our food, he carefully folded his napkin onto his plate and pushed it to the side.

"I'm assuming Marcus sent you."

"Yes."

"I've been expecting some type of communication after he warned us to go dark."

"He's worried about you."

Terrence's forehead crinkled.

"I went to communicate through our backdoor route, you know leaving a message in a draft email. Even that was shut down."

"They don't trust anything online. That's why they sent me."

He cocked his head. "Did something happen?"

There was no way to soften it.

"Leanne, Scott, Cameron, and Sam are all dead. I'm so sorry. Only you and Charlie—Storm—are still alive."

"Jesus. All four? Oh man," he said it in a low voice. "I didn't know their real names. Only their user names."

I gave him a second. He reeled back in his seat and put his palms on the table. He let out a low whistle and then closed his eyes and shook his head. When he opened his eyes again, he trained them on me and said, "What happened?"

I filled him in.

"The police are covering it up, but they were murdered. Charlie took off and is in hiding."

He bit his lip and didn't speak for a few seconds.

"I'm going to release the information," he said. His mouth was set in a firm line. "I'm going to shut them down. That bastard."

"VladTheImpaler?"

He nodded.

"What do you know about him?" I asked.

"Just that he's the founder of the website. He was Storm's boss—I guess you know her as Charlie. She was in his inner circle. He's the one who has been threatening her. He's the one who must've hired a hit man."

I nodded. "How do we get him?"

Terrence shook his head. "I don't know who he really is. His identity is secret."

"I think you better do what Charlie did," I said. "Leave town for a while."

"I can't go into hiding," he said. "I got a baby now. I can't leave her or my wife. We're a family."

"Take them with you."

"It's not like that. Gloria doesn't know what I do. She won't leave her mama, anyway. Her mama is older and sickly."

"Then you leave. The hit man is probably only after you."

As soon as I said it, I took it back. "I'm sorry. We can't assume that can we?"

"I'm not leaving them unprotected," he said. He stood, throwing down two twenties on the table. "Thanks for the warning. I appreciate it. My treat for your troubles."

I stood as well. "Terrence, these guys are bad motherfuckers."

"I got responsibilities now. I owe that to my daughter Shalina. I'm not going to leave her."

"That baby needs a daddy who is alive," I said.

He exhaled loudly. "I'll keep a watch out. I'll be careful."

It wouldn't be good enough.

"Can you at least take a trip somewhere as a family for a while? Until we figure out who is doing this?"

"I'm not going to run."

He clenched his jaw.

I was about to walk away. I'd tried my best. But then I asked to see his phone.

He hesitated for a second and then handed it to me.

"This one's new. Secure," he said. As if I would know any different.

I punched in my contact info and handed it back. "It's under Gia. If you change your mind. Or if you need anything."

He took it, nodded, and walked out.

I sank back into the booth. What now? I was worried about him and his little family. Sticking around was not going to end well for him.

After I called Darling and filled her in, I told her I was heading home for the night. I needed to pick Rosalie up at Danny's place. I was already hours past when I said I'd be there. I'd go back to Sam's apartment in the morning.

18

HE'D MAKE HIS MOVE SOON. THEY SAID TIME WAS MORE important than a clean job.

His first stop would be the girl's mother. He'd find out where she was and then make plans to travel. He didn't mind a little business trip to Europe.

And it would be good to be out of town if he had to take out the young man and his entire family.

But first he'd try the kidnapping. He regretted suggesting it. It didn't pay as well, and he'd have to put up with two other people invading his space.

He did more recon. He figured out the best time. There was a small window. It was when the neighborhood gangbangers were having their nightly basketball game around the corner. Most of the busybodies from the street were inside cooking dinner and, best of all, ShadowKing was still making his way home from work.

It'd be perfect.

19

"VLAD, WE GOT A PROBLEM." THE MESSAGE FLASHED ON HIS DARK screen.

Blake closed his eyes for a second before replying.

He had been up until four in the morning responding to troubleshooting emails, resolving disputes between sellers and dealers, and trying to flush out a few scam artists on the site who were fleecing his customers.

The money the site was raking in was phenomenal, but sometimes he wondered at what cost to his health? His stress level was through the roof. He didn't sleep. Barely remembered to eat. He felt an electric tension throughout his body 24/7—a constant low-thrumming anxiety that it would all go up in smoke any second. His opus, his legend, would crumble before he fulfilled his desire to change the world. He wanted to change the way drugs were treated in this country forever. Sure, there were a few murders that occurred along the way, but the thousands of lives he had probably saved by offering a viable alternative to street-level dealing offset that.

"What's the problem?" he typed.

"We've got a hole we need to plug." It was Carl
—MagnusOpus.

Again? It was his fucking amateur programming. He was
self-taught. He'd made mistakes.

"What's up?" he typed.

"We're leaking Bitcoin."

"How much?" He cringed writing it.

"Quarter of a million dollars." Carl wrote. "So far."

He nodded. It could've been worse.

"Who's getting them?" he wrote.

"Not sure. Maybe Storm."

"How soon can the hole be plugged?" he wrote.

"I'm close. Very close. But we're leaking about 5 bitcoin an
hour—that's $50,000 an hour—and it's going to take me another
hour at least to figure this out."

"Just do your best."

He logged out of the chat room. He wasn't in the mood for
chitchat.

20

DANNY LIVED IN AN APARTMENT WITHOUT A DOORBELL OR intercom system, so I either had to stand in the middle of the street below and yell his name or text him to let me in.

Since it was nighttime, I opted for texting.

He answered by poking his big head with the curly red hair out the window and waving. I heard the click of the door and let myself in, feeling suddenly tired as I trod the stairs to his floor.

The door to his apartment was open. The interior was dim—lit only by a few of Danny's glowing computer screens and the light from a small TV. Rosalie was curled up in Danny's round Papasan chair, covered in a quilt.

"She conked out a few hours ago."

I closed my eyes, instantly feeling guilty for being out so late.

"I was working." Like I did anything else. I knew I sounded defensive. I didn't have Danny watch Rosalie so James and I could go on a date, but now, come to think about it, there was nothing wrong with that, either. So why did I feel so guilty?

Danny didn't answer my lame comment and I appreciated it. I turned to him.

"Have you ever heard of PeopleUnited?"

"Sure," he said. "They're behind the city takeover."

I guess I shouldn't have been surprised.

"What about the Omega Six?"

"Yeah, they're going after the Night Fall website. Pretty ballsy."

"Do you know any of them personally?"

"I know Storm. But I know who all of them are. Come to think of it, I haven't seen any of the Six online lately."

I swallowed. Fuck me. The last thing I wanted to do was tell Danny that most of them were dead.

"Gia?" He sensed my turmoil.

"I'm investigating the murder of three, well, now four of them." I said.

"Oh shit," he said.

I paused and then said, "I'm so sorry, Danny."

His chin dropped, and he stared at the ground. "Damn," he said softly, nearly under his breath. I reached out to touch his shoulder but then drew my hand back.

He looked up. "What about Storm, I mean Charlie?"

"You know her real name?" I asked.

"Yeah. She's the only one I know in real life."

"She took off," I said, happy to share some good news. "She was smart. She's in hiding. Wait? How do you know her, anyway?"

His neck reddened. "We went to high school together in Oakland. She figured out who I was—my user name was something I'd done a presentation on in eighth grade—ZombieStar. She reached out and asked if it was me and I fessed up. Then she told me who she was. We've been sort of friends ever since."

"Small world," I said.

"Not to sound conceited, but when you are at our level...we

pretty much all know each other. At least by username. Who else is left? In the Omega Six?" he said.

"Terrence Hall. I mean ShadowKing."

"They killed everyone else?"

I swallowed again but nodded.

Danny closed his eyes.

"But ShadowKing's okay?"

"For now," I said.

"He's a good guy."

"Have you met him, too?"

He blushed. "Not in person or anything. He just seems cool online."

"I just met him. Asked him to go into hiding or at least take a trip, but he wouldn't listen to me."

I knelt by Rosalie and gently shook her shoulder. "Come on, Rosie. Time to go home."

She reached for me and then was in my arms, her warm body pressed against mine.

I lifted her up. She was petite for her age. With all my weightlifting and training, I could easily carry her. I hoisted her onto my hip. She wrapped her arms around my neck and buried her face in the hair on my shoulder. I turned back toward Danny.

I had an idea. "Would ShadowKing listen to you?"

Danny shook his head slowly. "Nah. I doubt it."

"Maybe you could try?" I asked. "He has a new baby and..." I trailed off. I hated feeling helpless.

Danny let us out, and I headed down the stairs to where I'd parked the Jeep. I'd quickly exchanged my bike for the Jeep in my garage a few blocks away before I headed over. I figured Rosalie would be too sleepy to walk home.

As I strapped her in the back, I felt a wave of anxiety. I

needed to get her home and to bed and figure out who was killing the Omega Six before they got to Terrence and Charlie.

I thought about that baby crying. That baby needed her daddy.

It was up to me to make sure he was around for the long haul.

21

THE SMALL FLAT WAS IN BERNAL HEIGHTS.

An iron gate led to the entrance.

The Cleaner waited across the street in his car, pulling his black fedora down low but, other than that, not doing anything to hide. His dark blue sedan blended in with the other parked cars on the road. He had his fake license plates on, so he wasn't worried about anyone calling him in and finding out who he really was.

Shortly before eight, the gate opened. A woman, wearing an oversized tank top with her hair pulled back and her cheeks flushed, turned and was fumbling to lock the gate behind her.

He jumped out, grabbing his go bag. In his other hand, he clutched a sheaf of papers. He was across the street in seconds.

"Ma'am, I'm looking for Charlotte Koleman. I'm a process server, and I need to serve her these papers."

The woman frowned. "What?"

"It's a matter of a car accident, I believe. She's being sued. Sorry to break the news. If you just let me deliver these, I can be on my way." He held up a fistful of papers. She frowned. "I can't give them to you. I have to deliver them right to her."

"I'm not sure what to tell you," she said. "She won't be back for a long time. Maybe months."

It was as if a switch was flipped inside him. In an instant, he had his forearm out, pressing against the woman's neck and pinning her to the wall of the building before he even realized it.

"Where is she?"

The woman's eyes were wide with fright. He released his hold slightly so she could speak.

"I don't know. In Europe somewhere. She moves to a new place every day so bastards like you can't find her."

He looked into her eyes. They shone with pure hatred, but she was telling the truth.

"Where was she last? Do you know that much?"

She pressed her lips tightly together.

"Tell me." He pressed his forearm across her neck even tighter. Her eyes bulged. Her face turned pink. He released his grip. "Tell me," he said it softer now.

She looked him dead in the eye and said, "You will have to kill me. I will never, ever tell you."

He believed her then too.

He jerked his arm, moving her body so it was against the gate, and he pressed until they were both inside. He drew the gun out of the holster hiding beneath his jacket.

"Lock the gate."

"No."

He only hesitated long enough to glance quickly around the street outside before he brought the gun up and across her temple. She sank to the ground in a soft heap.

He took the keys from outside the gate and locked it from the inside.

Tucking his gun back in its holster, he dragged the woman by the feet around the corner, behind the stairwell, and out of sight of the sidewalk. There was a small closet space there; he put her inside. He'd have to hurry before she awakened. On second thought, he didn't feel like hurrying.

When she said she'd die rather than tell him where her daughter was, he knew that she was telling the truth. A mother's instinct to protect a child is the only thing he'd ever encountered that could overcome the fear of pain and death. Torture was off the table. Which was too bad.

He reached into the black bag slung over his shoulder and attached the silencer to the gun. He left the woman slumped in the closet with a small hole in her forehead. He shut the door and, armed with her keys, went up to the flat on the second floor.

22

THE GIRL WITH THE PINK-STREAKED HAIR ROLLED HER EYES WHEN she saw me leaning against the building near the front door.

"Me again." I gave her my sweetest smile.

"Yeah. I know. Sam's dead. Cops already came and told me. Looked in his room."

"What did you do with his stuff?"

"Nothing," she said. "I haven't had time to throw it away. Cops said he didn't have any family to come get his shit. As soon as I have time, I'm trashing it all. I'm going to move into the master bedroom and rent out the other room. It's about time I had my own bathroom."

"Show me his room."

"Fuck you."

I gave her a look that pretty much told her I did whatever I wanted whenever the hell I wanted. She looked away first.

"Fine. But stay the fuck out of the rest of my place. His room only." She unlocked the front door, and I followed her up one flight of stairs. There she unlocked another door and swung it open. "First door on the right."

The master bedroom was sparse. It had a twin bed up

against one wall with a white pillow and a thin gray bedspread. Against the other wall was a mammoth desk that was empty.

"Where's his computer?"

"Cops took it."

"Bullshit."

I walked over and slammed her against the wall, my arm pressed against her neck. I was tired, hungover, and annoyed. And sick of her shit.

"Where?"

"I sold it. To a guy at work."

"Where do you work?"

"Diamonds."

It was a trendy restaurant in the area.

"Who did you sell it to?"

"Matt."

I let her go. She ran out of the room, swearing and mumbling under her breath. "I'm going to call the fucking cops. You're trespassing."

"You let me in," I yelled over my shoulder.

"Assault then."

"Whatever."

23

I'D HAD LUNCH AT THE RESTAURANT BEFORE PICKING ROSALIE UP at school. The food hadn't been bad. I'd ordered lettuce wraps and a coconut soup, much like tom kha gai. After eavesdropping enough to figure out Matt didn't work until the dinner shift, I left, still picking Rosalie up five minutes late.

It filled me with guilt to see her little worried face watching the door when I walked in.

"Sorry, baby," I said.

The teacher who had to wait with Rosalie was not smiling.

It might've had something to do with the fact that this was the fourth time this month I'd been late. Five minutes at the most, but still.

I couldn't figure out why other parents were never late. Was it some magical ability bestowed on natural parents? I mean, I wasn't really a parent, so maybe that was why. I had guardian-ship...but then I shook all that away. I wasn't ready to go there. The only thing I knew was that this little girl depended on me, and I'd let her down.

I crouched before her and took her hands in mine.

"You okay?"

She nodded, but I could see the tears she was holding at bay. "Were you worried?"

She bit her lip and nodded again.

"I'm so sorry. I think from now on you should bring your cell phone. That way you can call me if you're worried. Or better yet, I can call you and tell you when I'm running late."

The teacher made a small sound, and I realized she obviously didn't approve of me giving Rosalie her own cell phone to deal with my tardiness and irresponsibility.

I turned to the teacher—a diminutive woman wearing a flowered dress that reached her ankles and her long hair in a ponytail. "She needs to have her phone with her from now on. I promise she won't use it unless she has to, right Rosalie?"

"Right." I could see the tension drop away from Rosalie at the mention of the phone.

I could tell the teacher didn't approve. And I was sorry about that. She was a good teacher, and Rosalie adored her, but she didn't know what Rosalie had been through and why she needed a phone. Besides, Rosalie had a phone before. And it had saved my life when a man was trying to kill me and she'd called 911.

I'd dare say we were both alive today because of that phone.

———

LATER, at home, I made Rosalie macaroni and cheese for dinner, feeling like the worst Italian-American ever. But the kid loved the stuff.

As much as possible, I tried to coordinate it so the three of us ate dinner together as often as possible, even if we didn't eat the same food. Tonight, James was intent on grilling a salmon fillet on the roof, and since I was going back to Diamond's to confront Matt, I wouldn't be eating. Rosalie refused to even be in the same room as fish, so mac and cheese it was.

I carried Rosalie's bowl up to the rooftop along with a bowl of salad and some cut up fruit that I hoped imparted at least a small amount of nutrition to her meal.

The three of us sat around the large wooden table under the pergola. Even though it was September, I had to turn on the portable heaters. San Francisco was a fickle lover. Sometimes it was hot as Hades on the street below and yet, here on the rooftop, cool from the fog or an ocean breeze or both.

But it was worth it to watch the sunset. Long before the sun dipped to the horizon out of our view, it metamorphosed into a massive, glowing red orb and filled the sky with color.

"*Bellissima*," I said, sipping my wine and admiring the sunset.

James, who had his back to me and Rosalie, ignored my comment.

"How's the PI biz?" I said in an attempt to get him to interact with us. I knew he'd been out late working on some case.

"Fine. I'm getting better at following cheating husbands around," he said. His voice was thick with sarcasm. I felt bad for him. It wasn't exactly how he'd envisioned his PI business would go.

"You can be pickier about the cases you take on," I said.

He turned. A flash of anger spread across his face. "It's not like I'm being bombarded with clients wanting to hire me, Gia."

He was right. "It will take time, but word will spread."

He didn't respond. A sour taste filled my mouth. He was slowly but surely drawing away from me and from our life.

Ever since he'd been let go from the police department, James had struggled against feeling like he depended on me and my money. We both knew I had enough to last until Rosalie was a very old woman, but James needed to pay his own way. I understood. But I hated that it made him take on cases he loathed.

What really needed to happen was for us to nail the police chief. That was the main goal. I'd filled him in on the chief possibly covering up four murders in the city.

James scoffed. "He'll get away with it, just like he has with everything else."

"Not if I have anything to do with it."

But I was bluffing. I didn't know how to get the chief—legally that was. And that's all James would settle for.

James frowned. He was turning bitter and cynical the longer the chief walked the streets a free man. I didn't blame him, but it hurt my heart to see.

"We can talk about it later," I said and smiled. "Let's just enjoy this beautiful night."

He didn't answer. I could see by the set of his jaw that he was angry.

Rosalie scooted back her chair and raced to the edge of the roof, facing the sunset.

"I love it. I love red," she said. "It's my favorite color."

The anger seemed to fall off James as he turned to watch Rosalie.

It was the only thing lately that seemed to make him happy —being with that little girl. Lately, when it came to James, all I did was worry about the anger that lay simmering constantly just below the surface.

But I couldn't save him from himself.

What I *could* do was help keep Terrence and Charlie alive.

Away from my little rooftop fortress, people were dying. And more people were in danger of dying. I scooted my chair back and got ready to leave.

James barely said goodbye to me.

24

He stroked Midnight's sleek hairless body. She purred under his touch. Then she did something that rarely happened, she gave him a small lick with her rough tongue. It startled him so much, he flung her off the couch. She hissed and ran into the other room.

He chased after her. "I'm sorry. You just scared me. You just scared me."

It upset him more than he wanted to admit. But what he really didn't want to admit was that the small lick had turned him on. What kind of fucking creep gets turned on by an animal licking him. He started to laugh. Walking over to his counter, he checked his calendar. Yes. It was that. Jesus, a breeze would turn him on right then. He had counted the days since he last had sex. Fourteen days was way too long. For a second, he stood holding his phone, wanting to call Phoebe and tell her he was heading over to her house.

She would never argue. She would never say no. He was pretty sure that he was the only guy she'd ever fucked. She was so socially awkward that she barely spoke to anyone else. He'd met her one day in the market near his house. She was staring blankly at a row of cereal boxes. Like she was in a daze. He noticed that she had a firm ass and huge tits under her long skirt and baggy T-shirt. He bumped into her ass from behind, and she gave a small "Oh!" so he did it again. He got her number and they'd had sex regularly ever since. She lived with her mother, so he always had to sneak in the back door, which somehow made it more exciting. Phoebe became a wild woman in bed. Sometimes he marveled at his sex life. After years of having to pay for sex, just one encounter at the market had changed his life.

Just thinking of Phoebe made him horny, but he realized he'd have to wait. It was late and he had to stay on his game. He still had work to do. Once he was done with these two jobs, he would be loaded. He'd have enough money to take Phoebe on vacation if he wanted to. That would be his reward. He would take her somewhere away from her elderly mother's house and they could fuck all day and all night. Yes. That was a great plan.

25

I HEADED BACK TO THE RESTAURANT AROUND 8:00 P.M. AND requested a seat by the kitchen. It didn't take long to figure out who Matt was. He was a tall, lanky guy with greasy, slicked-back black hair, low-slung jeans with a chain looped from the wallet in his back pocket to the pocket in the front. His sneakers were the stupid expensive ones, a few hundred bucks for some rubber and canvas. He served the table beside me. My take on him was that he was surly. A rich kid whose parents made him wait tables in college on principle while they paid the rent on his fancy San Francisco apartment.

I nursed my second glass of wine until they flicked the closed sign on. Then I was gone in a heartbeat and across the street, waiting in a shadowy doorway, eyes on the side door. My Blackbird was parked nearby.

I eyed the few cars left on the street. A Toyota minivan. A Honda SUV. A Land Rover.

I didn't even need to see Matt come out and put the key in the door to know the Land Rover was his. I waited until he had rounded the corner before I hopped on my motorcycle. He led me to a fourteen-story building on the side of the 101 Freeway not far from the onramps to the Bay Bridge. I kept my bike idling down the street until his taillights dipped into the underground parking garage. Then I gunned it, my engine roaring as I raced toward the closing garage door. It slid shut right after I hopped off my bike. It was a fine line, balancing tailing someone close enough to stick to them while maintaining enough distance that you wouldn't be spotted. Tonight, I'd blown it. But as dumb luck would have it, the door started creaking open again. I dipped under it before the car coming down the road even reached the driveway.

Across the garage, I heard a door slam and saw Matt walking toward an elevator. I had to be in that elevator with him, but if I stepped inside he would wonder how the chick from his restaurant appeared suddenly beside him. I could possibly pull off surprise: "Hey, you live here too? Don't you work at Diamond's?" But I'd try something else first.

As I strode toward him and the elevator entrance, I shed my All Saints moto jacket, tossing it in a corner, hoping it didn't get grease on it. I fucking loved that jacket. Then in one swift motion, I pulled my thick, long hair up into a messy bun. It wasn't the best disguise, but it might just work.

I kept my eyes trained on Matt's back. He was standing in front of the elevator. I was still too far away. The elevator doors slid open. He stepped inside. The doors started to close.

"Wait!" I yelled. "Could you hold the door please?"

A foot appeared right before the doors sealed. A foot clad in fancy sneakers. And then a hand held the door higher up. By the time I reached the doors, they had opened, and I was face to face with Matt. He had an odd look on his face. At first, I worried he recognized me, but then I realized he was flustered and kept avoiding looking at my chest. I glanced down.

In ripping my leather jacket off, my off-shoulder top had slipped waaaay off to one side. And I wasn't wearing a bra. Oops.

I yanked the top up and scooted backward against the elevator wall. Taking my jacket off also meant the Ruger stuck in my back waistband would be more obvious. I wasn't ready for him to see that. Not yet.

"Floor?"

I glanced over and saw he'd hit the button for the fifth floor.

"Five." He met my eyes with a surprised look.

I raised an eyebrow. "What?" I said, acting nonchalant.

"You live on my floor?" His brows knit in consternation.

"I'm just visiting." I figured it was the easiest lie.

"Oh." Good. It also shut him up.

He still looked suspicious, frowning and working the skin on the inside of his mouth, chewing furiously. There was no reason for him to be acting this way. Most college kids would never even consider they were being followed. I wondered what his deal was.

"Who are you here to see?" he finally said.

"Why?" I held his gaze.

He squirmed. "I just wondered." He fidgeted even more. "I was going to go up to the rooftop hot tub later, and if you were here to visit a friend maybe you guys would want to come up. I'm going to break this open."

He extracted a bottle of red wine from a paper bag he'd been holding.

I wondered if he'd stolen it from the restaurant.

"I don't have a swimsuit."

"Oh."

"But maybe..."

His eyes widened. The elevator door opened. I turned toward him and backed into the hall. He stepped out after me, an eyebrow arched.

"Maybe. First I have to ask you about the computer your pink-haired friend sold you."

"What?" He blinked in confusion.

"Come on, Matt. Make this easy for me."

He backed up, but the elevator doors had closed. "Who are you?"

"Nobody you need to worry about. I just need to see that computer. Probably take it. Don't worry, I'll pay you for it."

"What the—?" He was much taller than me and outweighed me by probably thirty pounds, but he backed up against the elevator as if he thought he would magically melt into it.

"Matt. This is important. I wouldn't ask, but there are people's lives at stake."

He shook his head as if I were a bad dream or a hallucination.

"Come on, now," I said, throwing my hand out. "Let's go get the computer. We're burning daylight, sailor."

He didn't move. He reached for his cell phone.

"Who are you calling?"

His head was still dipped down as I reached over and yanked the phone out of his hand. He'd only gotten as far as punching in the nine and a one.

"No need to call the cops. If you cooperate, I'll be gone in ten minutes."

"No." His face had grown red, a blush spreading up from his neck to his cheeks.

"Give me your keys," I said. "And then we can play it two ways. I can either try all eight doors on this floor until we find yours or you can just tell me which apartment it is."

"No way." He scowled as he said it.

I exhaled exaggeratedly. I reached behind me and took out my gun. I kept it aimed at the ground. "Matt. You have a choice here. Are you going to make this easy and quick, or hard and drawn-out?"

He closed his eyes for a second.

"How do I know you aren't going to get into my apartment and kill me?" he said.

"Why would I kill you?"

He yanked at his hair and said in a screechy voice, "How the fuck do I know? Why are you even here? None of this makes sense."

"Sure it does, Matt. You play with fire, you get burned. You buy stolen shit, there's a consequence. It's basic as fuck."

He glared at me.

"Which door is yours?" I backed up as I said it, giving him room to move. I kept the gun at my side, pointed at the floor.

He closed his eyes again. Then took a step to the left. He paused.

"Keep going, sailor."

"How do I know you aren't going to kill me?" he said again.

"Because I don't want to kill you, Matt. I just want the computer."

I yawned. He was such a bore.

He led me to the fourth door on the left. His hands were shaking as he unlocked it. He pushed the door open. "I'm not going in with you. The computer is in the living room. You can't miss it. It's not set up yet. It's just sitting there on a table."

"Good boy," I said. "But I need to make sure you don't alert the authorities before I get out of here. Why don't you go lock yourself in the bathroom if you don't believe I won't hurt you."

He stared at me.

"Go on now," I said, gesturing with the gun. He scurried inside. I followed. He ducked into a small room off the hall, and I heard the door lock. "That's it, Matt. Everything is going to be just fine."

I was scanning the apartment as I said it.

Sleek furnishings. Definitely not from Ikea.

Bolted to the wall was a massive TV screen that was equally

as large as the plate glass window overlooking the glittering lights of the skyscrapers in downtown. *Jesus.* The apartment wasn't even big enough for it. You'd have to scoot back against the far wall so you didn't get a headache watching it. Like sitting in the front row of the movie theater. Fun when you're nine. Not so great when you're an adult.

The massive monitor sat on a coffee table next to a hard drive tower. But first, I needed to make sure Matt stayed in the bathroom until I left. Eyeing the hard drive, I thought of my bike downstairs. It would be an interesting ride back to the Tenderloin. I scanned the apartment, hollering, "Doing okay in there, Matt? I'm almost done here."

There was a heavy oak bookshelf not far from the bathroom. By putting all my weight into it, I managed to scoot it over in front of the door. The scraping had Matt concerned.

"What are you doing?" His voice sounded teary.

"Don't worry," I said, panting with the effort. "Almost done here and then you can go on about your life. By the way, I'm not sure what you were planning to tell the cops. Were you going to say that a woman is here demanding you return stolen shit you bought? Possession of stolen goods is a felony in the state of California."

I heard him groan.

It was probably a misdemeanor, but poor little rich boy Matt wouldn't know that.

Once the bookshelf was in place, I threw open a closet near the front door. It contained a bunch of hiking gear. Perfect. I grabbed some bungee cords. It would look stupid, but I could strap the hard drive to my back. But then I spotted a massive backpack near the back of the closet and tossed the cables on the ground. I held the bag before me, eyeing it and looking back into the living room at the hard drive.

"Hey Matt, I'm going to leave here in a few minutes. Start

counting to one hundred. And remember, possession of stolen goods is a felony. I'd be happy to explain to police that I was here retrieving Sam's property to give back to his family."

Another lie. Oh well.

Less than seven minutes later I was on my bike heading home, sporting an obnoxious orange backpack.

It would've been six minutes, but I had to go back into the garage to retrieve my All Saints jacket. I loved that thing. I left Matt's cell phone propped on his hood. I figured he could probably knock the bookshelf over with a little effort, but it would at least take him a bit longer to sound the alarm than if he simply had to open the door and walk out. Chances were good, though, that he wasn't going to say jack shit about my visit.

Poor Matt. I hoped he'd learned his lesson about buying stolen goods.

BLAKE WAS FREAKING OUT.

Carl had plugged the hole, but less than twenty-four hours later, the site had been hacked again. It was down. Incapacitated. Right before it went down, Carl had received a message demanding 200 bitcoin—about 2 million dollars.

Someone besides Omega Six had attacked. And demanded a ransom.

"Advise," Carl typed.

"Pay it. We're losing that much each hour the site is down," Blake wrote back.

Rosalie was in her room asleep when I stepped into the loft. Django poked his head out of her door, growling slightly until he saw it was me, and then his nose disappeared as he backed up and went back to bed.

I'd lost my dog to Rosalie.

But she needed him more than I did.

That dog loved her. He treated her like she was his child. It filled my heart with joy.

James was at our dining room table, his wheelchair pulled up to his laptop. A cup of coffee still had steam coming from it.

I leaned over and kissed his neck. "Looks like you don't plan on sleeping tonight," I said, nodding at the coffee.

"Check this out," he said. Relief filled me. He didn't sound angry anymore.

I crouched down so I could see his screen better. It was a picture of the police chief having dinner with a brown-haired woman.

"Who's he with?"

"Not his wife."

"Nope. Not his wife."

I reached over and began to rub his shoulders, giving him a massage, and then leaned down to gently kiss the back of his neck. I suddenly wanted to have sex with him desperately.

He pushed me away without a word and without even looking up from his computer, as if I were a pesky fly.

I drew back, both shocked and hurt. I tried not to cry as I got ready for bed. Once I was under the covers, I stared into the darkness, wondering where it had all gone so wrong.

I knew I'd been gone lately—absent physically and mentally as I tried to figure out how to stop a killer. Tonight, I'd wanted to go straight over to Danny's with the hard drive I'd just recovered, but I knew I needed to be home at least one night. I'd already missed Rosalie's bedtime, as it was.

Maybe that's why James was pushing me away. I didn't blame him.

Even though I was physically there, my mind was racing. I needed to stop that assassin before more people ended up dead.

———

"I don't want to go to school today." Rosalie stomped her foot.

I lifted my coffee mug up to my mouth to hide my smile. It was nice to see her acting a little bratty. It meant she was comfortable. For the few months she'd been here, she'd been timid and almost subservient, as if she were afraid we would send her back to Guatemala to live with a distant relative. Right now, the only relative she knew was some distant aunt.

I'd told her a few times that she could disagree with us, get angry with us, even stomp her feet and yell, and we still would want her around. Finally, it seemed she believed me.

We still had an hour until we had to leave for school. James had left earlier. He'd barely said goodbye to me. I was too hurt by the way he acted the night before to say much either.

I crouched down before Rosalie. "You don't want to go to school? Why not?"

My voice was even.

"Courtney said I talk funny."

"She did, huh?"

Rosalie crossed her arms across her chest and nodded, her lips pressed together.

"Did she say it mean, or did she just say it."

Rosalie's forehead scrunched up. "Just said it."

"Do you think she was trying to be mean?"

Again she paused, looking off in the distance, remembering. "I don't know."

"Do you think it's because you have an accent, or was it because of something you'd said, some word you used?"

"Accent. My r's sound different than when the teacher says it."

"Did it hurt your feelings that she said that to you?"

She pressed her lips even tighter together and nodded.

"I'm sorry." I pulled her in a hug. "I understand that it's hard to be new to a school and to a country and to a language. You want to fit in and be like everyone else, but here's the thing, you're so wonderful *because* you aren't like everyone else. That's one of the parts of you I love—that tiny, tiny accent you have. It makes what you say sound so beautiful to me."

She gave me a look, unconvinced.

"What do you think Courtney would say if you told her saying that hurt your feelings?"

Rosalie shrugged.

"Do you think it would help?"

Again, the slight lift of her shoulders.

"Wanna try and see what she says? It's important to tell people how you feel if they say something you don't agree with. Okay?"

"Okay."

"Should we get ready for school?"

"Okay."

————

AT THE SCHOOL, I wanted to linger, worried that I'd set Rosalie up for more hurt feelings or conflict with another kid, but I knew I had to let go. So I gave her a kiss on the forehead and turned to walk away, leaving her to hang up her backpack and get on with her day. I had tucked her cell phone into her backpack pocket, though, telling her only to call me if there was an emergency.

As soon as I got home, I loaded up Sam's hard drive to take it over to Danny's. He'd said unless it was encrypted, we could probably garner some information from it.

On the walk over, Darling called. "Charlotte's mother was murdered yesterday."

My heart sunk. I remembered the middle-aged woman's face as she spoke about Charlie. That young woman was going to be devastated. There was no way she wouldn't blame herself for her mother's death.

I knew. I had nothing to do with my own parent's murder, and still I found ways to blame myself. It's what people did. They looked for would'ves, should'ves, and could'ves when someone they loved died.

Knowing Charlie was going to go through this, too, sent anger surging through me.

There was a killer out there and, apparently, he or she was killing anybody who got in the way. I'd been tasked with trying to protect these people and, so far, I'd failed.

28

He was a failure. A loser. Just like everyone had always said.

Back in his house, he yanked the blinds closed. One set of blinds tangled, and he angrily tried to straighten it out. It was caught up in the fine cords. He tugged. It remained stuck. He tried again.

Fury filled him. He ripped at the cord, and the entire set of blinds clattered to the floor. He saw red. He screamed and shouted, spittle flying as he waved his hands around in the air. He roared in anger and grabbed the side of his bookcase, sending it plunging to the ground. In his red haze, he ran into his closet and buried his face in a stack of his neatly folded sweaters stacked on a hanging shelf. He screamed. He felt something at his feet and began to stomp in fury. Only when she screeched in pain did he realize he'd hurt Midnight. He crumpled to the ground and cradled her in his lap. She licked him with her scratchy tongue.

Holding her calmed him down.

Despite tearing apart the flat where that girl and her mother lived, he'd found no signs of where the girl was hiding out in

Europe. He was ready to hop on a plane, but he needed to know where to even begin to look.

There wasn't a single computer in the home. Nor a smart phone. Or iPad. Not even an eReader. The mother still used an old-fashioned landline. Even the TV was out of date. He'd rifled through all the paperwork to be found in the house, but there still was no sign of where Charlie was hiding. No travel documents or receipts. No phone numbers scribbled on a piece of paper. Nothing.

He'd failed.

He had to go onto Night Fall to report his failure. It was the first time he'd failed to complete a job since he'd gone freelance five years ago. It would be a permanent black mark on his flawless record. It would affect his future jobs. It would mean he might go longer stretches in between work. Having to wait longer to kill would slowly drive him insane. It was unacceptable.

Someone would pay for this. He would make sure someone paid.

But first he'd finish the rest of the job. He had one assignment right here in town.

He grabbed his go bag. Time to move.

29

I LUGGED SAM'S HARD DRIVE UP TO DANNY'S APARTMENT, AND HE immediately got to work.

Sitting in the Papasan chair, I tried to think about anything besides what was going on with me and James. If he didn't want to have sex with me, something had gone terribly wrong. Even when we weren't getting along, we couldn't keep our hands off one another. Something had definitely changed. My stomach roiled with nervousness.

"Aha," Danny said looking up from his bank of computer monitors. "I think I found something. MatadorRed, or Sam as you knew him, set up an attack on Night Fall—a prescheduled attack. Stand by." Danny's head whipped to the monitor beside the one he was looking at.

He pulled a keyboard toward him and started typing furiously, keeping his eyes glued on the second monitor. A black command box appeared with a flashing cursor in the corner.

"Boom!"

"What? What? Explain." I leaped up from my seat and leaned in, staring at the computer screen.

"He took Night Fall down!"

"What? That's Night Fall?"

"Yep."

"Fuckity fuck fuck!"

"Damn right," Danny said and turned to me with a grin. "He's asking for a ransom before he lets it go. And he says one of the conditions is that they back off Charlie permanently."

"But..." *He's dead.* I wondered if this meant the end of the site.

"This is great news," Danny said. "Best thing that could've happened."

"Explain."

"We use this to lay a trap for them. When they pay we can sneak in through a back door."

I was skeptical. "You think they'll go for it."

"Yep. He's not asking a lot. Not for a site that makes that much money."

"How are you going to sneak in?"

Danny looked at me and raised an eyebrow. He knew I wouldn't understand.

"Oh, never mind," I said. "Just do it."

An hour later, I was lazing in the Papasan, keeping an eye on Danny and the monitors, but from my viewpoint, it didn't seem like anything had happened or changed. But Danny stood up and pushed in his chair.

"Done. We're in."

"What?" I sat up.

"Night Fall paid up. When they did, it opened a back door they didn't know about. I was able to sneak into the admin section of the site."

"What does that mean?"

"I released the hold on the site. It's back up. Right now, I'm just snooping around. I'll keep you posted."

"Did they agree to back off of Charlie?"

Danny shook his head. "Ignored it completely. I let it go so we could get inside."

He went to the refrigerator and pulled out a cold pizza box and started to put some pieces on a plate.

I stared at him.

He looked back. "Hungry?"

"No. Hey, not to be ungrateful, but you seem pretty relaxed about this. Don't you think you should be on the computer right now trying to find out who the killer is?"

He looked up at me. "I'm monitoring everything. Vlad is offline. I've got a program running through all the back chats in the admin section looking for the conversation where he took out the hit. It will ping as soon as the program finds it."

"Okay then."

He looked at his large Star Wars clock on the wall. "Go get Rosalie from school. I'll text you when I hear something."

I liked this confident, take-charge side of Danny. I gave him a small salute at the door.

"Aye-aye, captain."

30

"I was wrong."

I'd only just returned home from picking up Rosalie from school and was making her pasta for dinner when my cell rang. James didn't even look up from his computer as I raced over to the table, thinking it was Danny. It was Hall on the other end of the line.

I froze.

"What happened?"

"I was wrong. They took my baby."

His words sunk in, and my face turned icy cold.

"Where are you?"

"At my house. You gotta help me. You gotta do something." He was shouting, his voice frantic, panicked and on edge.

"Be there in ten."

I raced toward the elevator.

"Gia?" It was James. He'd said about two words to me since he got home. We were playing the silence game. It was getting old. When Rosalie went to bed tonight, we were going to have a serious talk. I was done with this bullshit.

I shook my head. "I'll explain later," I said as the elevator doors closed. The last thing I saw was Rosalie sitting near her doll house holding a doll. She sat motionless, her hand frozen in the air, her eyes on me.

Fuck. I was the worst person for her to live with. Zero stability. Drama. It was not okay. I couldn't change, and she deserved better. A stable home life. Hell, James deserved that as well.

I was meant to be alone. It was the only way I could live. This domestic shit was wrong.

In the garage, I punched the code into the keypad on the gun safe built into the wall. I took out my small Beretta Pico and tucked it into my waistband. Then I grabbed my Ruger and stuck that in a shoulder holster before yanking my motorcycle jacket on.

I zoomed out of the garage and headed toward the stadium and Hall's apartment.

He was pacing the sidewalk out front when I turned the corner onto his street. I drove right up onto the sidewalk in front of his open door. I parked and yanked my helmet off at the same time I reached for my gun and followed him into the open door.

I was cautious, holding my gun in front of me, but then dropped the gun to my side. The apartment was clearly empty.

31

THE WOMAN WAS CROUCHED IN THE CORNER OF THE BATHTUB when he unlocked the door. Her eyes were wide. Her shirt was lifted slightly, and the baby was suckling at her breast.

He turned away in disgust.

He plopped the plastic water pitcher down on the counter along with some crackers. It would keep her alive. Before he backed out, he gave another glance around the bathroom. There was nothing she could use as a weapon. He'd tried to tear off the towel racks, but they were firmly in place in the wall. He'd taken out everything from the small cabinet under the sink and cleared the counter off, even removing the small porcelain soap dish in case she had the dumb idea to throw it at him.

But really, he wasn't worried. She was so concerned about her baby, she wouldn't risk the child getting hurt while trying to fight him. He'd initially planned to march her to his car at gunpoint. But as soon as he had the baby in his arms, she was his bitch.

She'd sat in the backseat weeping and moaning but hadn't tried to escape.

He'd ordered her to put the blindfold on and then marched her up to his apartment. And then into the bathroom.

Before he left, his nose wrinkled. What was that smell?

Then he saw the diaper on the baby. It was soggy.

"Do something about that," he said, gesturing to the diaper.

She struggled to speak and then lifted her shoulders, her eyes darting around.

He'd left her untied in the locked bathroom. He hadn't made her sit in the tub, but she'd crawled in there on her own. It was the furthest spot from the door. So maybe that was why. Or maybe she just was sleeping.

Whatever. He didn't care.

He was just waiting for orders to torture her. Or get rid of her and the brat.

It wouldn't be the worst job he'd ever had, but definitely not the best one either. He would have to figure out how to get rid of both bodies. It wouldn't be easy. But with the money he'd been promised, it would be worth it. He'd kill her and then leave this disgusting apartment in this disgusting city full of degenerates and have enough money to start fresh somewhere else. Maybe South America? Maybe Peru? Maybe he could prey on people engaging in debauchery in Brazil. He could get a beat-up car at the border that wouldn't attract any attention and then just keep driving until he felt like stopping. Maybe he could convince Phoebe to come with him. They could live simply but well.

He knew that in some countries, his assassination skills were very valuable. As long as he had a laptop and access to the dark web, he could find work anywhere. He wondered why on earth he'd stuck around here so long. Stupid. Even the people who had hired him for this job were stupid. Why would the morons at Night Fall ever had contacted him directly? That's supposed to be why there was a middleman—to keep a distance between the person paying for the contract and the person fulfilling the contract. That's what The Patriot was supposed to do.

As soon as he completed this job and got paid, he'd take off and never step foot in this liberal, piece-of-shit city again. It was only a matter of time. He couldn't wait.

Bored while he waited for orders to begin torturing the woman, he flipped on the TV.

His eyes nearly popped out when he saw the picture on the screen. It was The Patriot. But underneath the photo it said that the short-haired man was the San Francisco Police Chief.

Grabbing the remote, he cranked the volume. He sat there in shock as the newscaster talked about how the police chief was trying to get funding for a helicopter but that a hacker group had taken over the city website until the city council agreed to vote against the funding.

He grabbed his laptop and logged onto the public chat room in Night Fall. His hands were shaking. This was so fucked up. The police chief had paid him to kill people. Unbelievable.

But the craziest part was that the chief knew that The Cleaner might know who he was. *And he didn't care.* That was why they were in Hunter's Point. All those cops? All the chief's men. He'd never heard of such a corrupt official.

For a second he wondered if he should be wary of dealing with the Patriot. What if it were some massive sting operation? But that couldn't be right. The chief had paid him for the hits. He was culpable. Something was very, very wrong. Right as the Cleaner thought that, he noticed something odd on his computer. His cursor moved. Without him touching it. Quickly he clicked open his task manager window. It showed there were four programs running that showed someone else had remote access.

He clicked on an anti-virus, anti-hacker program he'd bought. From Night Fall. He'd installed it to show if anyone had hacked into his computer. Shit. Shit. Shit. It showed someone was on his laptop and was downloading all its contents. He quickly popped off a message in the Night Fall public room and then shut down his computer, his heart pounding. If they were on his laptop, they would be able to trace his IP address and where he was. Right then. He shoved his laptop in his go-bag and was out the door in sixty seconds.

32

I surveyed Hall's place from the doorway. There were no signs of a struggle. Lamps weren't smashed. Furniture wasn't overturned. What had been destroyed had been done purposefully, methodically.

A desktop computer was destroyed—the huge monitor shattered, the hard drive in smithereens as if a sledgehammer had been taken to it. Papers from the desk were flung around the room. I saw a smear of blood on the corner of a tall table near the front door but tried not to stare or examine it.

I could picture it: The assassin barges in with some type of weapon, points it at the woman and uses it to destroy the monitor. Maybe he struck her with the gun as soon as she opened the door, which would explain the blood. But it would've had to have been a light tap. He wouldn't want her unconscious because he would have to drag her to his vehicle. Maybe just enough to send her to her knees.

I wondered where the baby was when he came in.

"When did you last speak to your girl?"

"About ten minutes before I got home."

"What did she say about your baby? Was she holding her? Was she napping?"

"It was naptime." He blushed. I cocked my head. He explained. "I was rushing home because we like to, um, take advantage of naptime, if you know what I mean."

"Got it," I said. "So the baby was likely sleeping. Does she sleep in her crib during naptime?"

"Yes."

I glanced toward the bedroom door. I could see a few inches of the crib.

His wife had probably flung open the door expecting Terrence. Got hit. Crumpled. Killer knew she wouldn't leave without the baby, so he probably walked right in and grabbed the kid first. Then at some point destroyed the monitor and hard drive. Terrence said his laptop was missing, so the killer must've taken time to grab that, too.

Once he had the baby, the woman was putty in the killer's hands. He could order her to his car, and she would go without question. That baby made her defenseless as fuck.

Even having Rosalie living with us for a few months made me feel more vulnerable than I'd ever felt in my life. And she was a tough little kid. A helpless baby would reduce me to a puddle. Good reason to avoid having kids.

I took one last look around.

"Let's go," I told Terrence and walked outside. He followed and watched as I strapped on my helmet and threw one leg over to straddle my bike.

"What?" He looked dazed and like he'd just been punched. "We need to find Gloria and Shalina."

"Get your car. We're going to Berkeley. We've got to find this guy, and I think your friends are the only ones who can track him on the dark web. He's a hired assassin. His work is too professional. Someone hired him online. We're going to find him. And find your girl and your baby."

"We don't need to go to the East Bay for that. But I will need some equipment," he said, his eyes narrowing. I saw anger there. Good. It was better than the sheer terror on his face when I first showed up.

"What do you need."

"They destroyed my desktop and took my laptop, but that's okay, it's encrypted and booby-trapped. But I need something powerful—preferably a bank of computers."

I smiled. "No problem."

33

I STOPPED MY BIKE ABOUT A BLOCK AWAY FROM DANNY'S apartment and kept it idling with one of my boots planted on the ground. Terrence stopped behind me. I held up a finger to indicate I needed a second.

I texted Danny, explaining the situation. "You cool with this? With me bringing him up?"

My phone screen remained blank for a second and my heart pounded. Danny's social awkwardness broke my heart. He was such a salt-of-the-earth guy; he deserved to have a thriving social life in person, not just friends online. I'd seen him blossom with Rosalie, though. Maybe meeting Terrence in person would be a good thing. Or maybe not.

"I'll help," he finally texted back.

"See you in thirty seconds," I wrote.

———

"DANNY'S one of the best people I've had the pleasure of meeting in this town," I said over my shoulder as we headed up the stairs.

"Cool," Terrence said. "Just grateful he's gonna help."

On the top floor, Danny's door was propped open.

"Hey guy," I said, slipping inside with Terrence behind me.

Danny had his back to us, sitting at a long table cluttered with a bank of computers. He was typing and didn't look over as he said, "Hey."

Terrence was instantly at his side and gave a low whistle. "Impressive, man."

Danny nodded without looking over.

"Hey, this is Terrence."

"One sec," Danny said. A few seconds later, he pushed the keyboard aside and swiveled his chair around. "Hi. We got into the Night Fall site a few hours ago. I'm running a few programs right now looking for info on the kidnapper. I'm also searching chats for mention of him."

"Thanks," Terrence said. He gestured to a chair next to Danny's. "You mind?"

Danny shook his big head, his curls bobbing.

He pointed at a monitor to Terrence's left. It showed some text with usernames beside them. "Recognize any of these users?" Danny asked.

Terrence scooted his chair over and squinted.

"Scroll down," Danny said.

Terrence did. Then he stopped, taking his finger off the mouse. "This guy. I've seen him poking around on our site before."

Danny rolled his chair over and pulled the keyboard in front of him. "Let's see what he's been up to and who he really is."

A half hour later, some information popped up that Danny printed out. "He's local."

"Bingo," Terrence said.

"Let's run possible connections to him."

I stood behind the two men wishing I could help. And, also, wishing I still smoked. This hacking stuff was boring to watch.

An hour later, I was slumped in Danny's Papasan chair when both men shouted:

"Holy shit!"

"Right here."

I popped out of my seat. "You got someone?"

Terrence nodded. He stood and clenched his hands into fists. "There's a guy. Down by the stadium. He might be good for this. Right after Vlad told MagnusOpus to take out the hit, Magnus started chatting with this guy. The Patriot. They weren't talking about murder and kidnapping. In fact, they were talking about the Giants, but that doesn't mean anything. It's all code."

"Who is this guy?"

"The Patriot is the middleman. The hitman is called The Cleaner. I just took over his computer remotely. I'm starting to download everything. Wait. I got the IP location!"

He reeled off the address of an apartment near the Sunset District.

"Let's go," I said and grabbed my leather jacket and motor-cycle helmet.

"Oh shit!" Danny was still seated. "He knows we're on to him. He just started deleting his accounts. Shit! Go! Go! Go!"

Danny stood. I'd never seen him this excited.

Terrence was already at the door. "Thanks, man," he shouted over his shoulder.

And then he was gone. I raced after him, blowing a hasty kiss to Danny. "Thanks, sailor!"

His cheeks flushed red before I was even out the door.

34

Blake rubbed his eyes. He'd fallen asleep in his desk chair. After he woke, he saw he'd been tagged in at least a dozen messages on the site's public forum. They all said the same thing. They were from the hitter. The Cleaner. Blake could hardly believe his eyes.

"I've been made," the message said. "Delete everything on the site that involves me. And I figured out who the Patriot is. Do you know who he is? Was this a trick? A trap? If I go down, I'll take you all with me. Baby mama alive."

Blake was furious. The guy had popped onto a public forum on the site and messaged him, *threatened* him. The first thing Blake did was delete the message. This was a *public* chat room. What was this guy thinking? He messaged him privately. "Dude. Calm down. Patriot is with us."

The hitter was *not* supposed to even know there was a Night Fall connection. Night Fall was supposed to be the vehicle where he was contracted for hit jobs, not the one hiring him. What the heck? He was only supposed to communicate through The Patriot. This was a disaster.

While he waited for the hitter to respond, Blake messaged

Carl. "Why is the hitter messaging me. What's going on? He's only supposed to communicate through The Patriot. How does he even know to message me?"

He was starting to feel hysterical. He waited, feeling his face grow hot with anger. The anxiety rose from his gut to his throat and could feel the pulse in his jaw throbbing. This was bad. Really bad.

He'd said the baby mama was alive. Did that mean the baby was dead? Or were both of them alive?

Shoot. Shoot. Shoot. If the mother was alive, she could possibly identify the hitter. Blake had to break all ties with him immediately. He went into the admin section of Night Fall and started by deleting every post by The Patriot or The Cleaner. But he wasn't sure if that would be enough. He needed advice. He needed help.

Where the heck was Carl?

35

WHEN WE GOT DOWNSTAIRS, TERRENCE WAS STANDING AT MY BIKE instead of at his car. I'd strapped my helmet on as I raced down the stairwell.

"Hop on," I said when I saw him.

We were down the block in seconds, his grip on my waist tight.

"You're packing?" He had to shout.

I nodded. No use denying it when he'd clearly felt the gun in my waistband.

I slowed for a corner at the last second, remembering he didn't have a helmet.

It was closing in on midnight. Fog had seeped onto the streets, making downtown feel even more desolate and deserted than usual. Within five minutes we were at the address Danny had given us. I nearly laid the bike down rounding the corner.

"Jesus," Terrence said, hopping off onto the sidewalk.

"Sorry." We were both at the apartment building's door. It was unlocked. I paused at the entrance. "Why don't you circle round and see if there is a back way out of here," I said.

"No way. I'm going in. Apartment twenty-seven."

He disappeared inside, and I started round the side of the building, relieved Terrence took the bait.

If the assassin was on to us—and it sounded like he was—he wasn't coming out the front. Terrence didn't have a weapon. But I did.

The side of the building was sheer brick wall. A tall fence blocked off the rear where I could see a parking lot. That's where he'd come out if he was still here.

I tucked my gun back into its holster and scaled the fence, cursing as my jeans caught on the barb wire at the top. I'd laid my leather jacket across the wire, but when my leg swung wide, I felt a sharp prick and heard fabric rip. But then I was on the other side, grabbing my jacket and pulling it back on as I raced for the door I saw in the shadows. I was nearly there when I heard a click. I threw myself against the wall only a few feet away from the entrance.

The parking lot was shadowy and dimly lit. The one street-light was at the far side near the gate leading out of the lot. Even so, I could tell immediately this was our guy. He had on a ball cap pulled low, a bulky jacket, and was carrying a large duffel bag. I could tell it was heavy—it nearly hung to the ground, and he seemed to struggle with it as he emerged from the doorway. It wasn't packed with gym clothes, that was for sure.

"Stop!" I yelled and pointed my Ruger at him. His head whipped my way. At the same time, his hand came up and sprayed me with something—mace or tear gas or pepper spray —that stung like burning fire on my face. It felt as if I had a painful sunburn and someone was holding a blowtorch a millimeter away from my skin. The scorching feeling was in my eyes, nose, and mouth. It sent me crashing to my knees, blind and gasping for air. My eyes instantly swelled shut, and I felt my throat seem to shrink as I crouched on the ground, struggling to suck air into my lungs. I was simultaneously throwing wild punches in case he came for more.

I could feel every thrum of my heartbeat pulse painfully in my jaw and neck and finally realized the footsteps I heard were running away from me. I scrambled to my feet, but no matter how hard I tried to force my eyes open, I was in the dark. I tucked my gun into my waistband. It took both hands to pry my right eyelid open a slit.

I lunged in the direction of the footsteps, holding my eyelid open. I heard a car start across the lot. I was running now, able to see enough to avoid crashing into one of the many vehicles parked in the lot. I reached the other side just in time to lunge for the tailgate of a small, black compact car. As it sped out of the lot, I tried to see the license plate number, but the car had turned. I saw a man in a ball cap, and the car was gone. I ran into the street and watched it disappear.

I stopped and put my hands on my knees. The pain in my lungs and the burn on my face took over. I made a small whimpering sound and was immediately mad at myself for it. It was just pepper spray for fuck's sakes, not a bullet.

I turned to look back at the building. In one corner was a small garden. I heard the sound of trickling water and ran over. I dunked my face in the small fountain, blinking furiously to try to rinse the burn away. At first, with my face submerged, I felt a small measure of relief, but then felt like I was drowning. I whipped my head up, my hair on the sides of my face dripping wet.

As soon as my face met the air, it began to burn again. I wanted to curl up in the fetal position. But I needed to go find Terrence.

After one more dunking, the pain subsided enough that it no longer took my breath away. Now it just felt like a horrendously painful sunburn. And I could now see slits of light instead of complete black. I used both hands again to pry my eyelids open and headed for the backdoor. As I did, I heard the sound of sirens in the distance.

There were a few possible scenarios awaiting me upstairs:

Terrence found his family inside the apartment. Alive. Dead. Hurt.

Only one way to find out.

HE'D ONLY JUST MADE IT OUT.

But he wouldn't go far. He had to know who this woman was and how they'd tracked him.

After circling the block, he swung around to the front of the apartment building and parked a few doors down. He broke into the office building across the street just as the police cars arrived.

THE COPS WHO RESPONDED TO TERRENCE'S 911 CALL DREW DOWN on me in the hall when I exited from the stairwell with my gun in my hands. At that point, I could see a little bit and realized putting my hands up with my Ruger in them might not be a smart move, but I had little choice.

As soon as they'd seen me emerge, one of them shouted "Gun!" and chaos ensued.

That's how James had been paralyzed. Someone had shouted that he had a gun, and before anyone could check, two cops had fired and he'd lost the use of his legs.

I heard Terrence shout, "She's my friend."

Only then did the four cops pointing service revolvers at me, chill. I could see much better now, about as good as if I were squinting.

"Put the gun down."

"Got it." I very slowly lowered my arm, keeping the gun pointed away from anyone and set it on the floor in front of me. "Easy, cowboy," I said in a low voice. "I'm his friend."

The cop who had shouted was lanky with close-shorn brown hair and slight acne on his cheeks. Baby cop. Chock full of young man testosterone. As soon as my gun hit the floor, he kicked it away and slammed me up against the wall. He was about to pat me down when another office came over with Terrence.

"Ten-four, Morrison. She's with the family."

He let go but he was still only a few inches away from me. The adrenaline was obviously still surging through his body, so it took him a second of heavy breathing and staring into my eyes before he nodded and backed off.

"Can I have my gun?" I was annoyed.

"Where's your permit?"

I scowled. "I don't know. Can't you run it in the system if I give you my name?"

The cop shook his head. Another cop scooped up my gun and stuck it in a plastic bag.

"Come down to the station when you've found your carry-and-conceal permit."

"Fuck you." I didn't mention that I had the Beretta in my waistband. None of his business.

The elevator dinged open, and two EMT's emerged with a stretcher.

I looked at Terrence.

"We got here in time," he said.

"Thank God."

I stood against the wall of the hall as the EMTs made their way into the apartment.

"Can I go back in now?" Terrence asked the cop near the door.

"Give the sergeant another second to talk to them. He's hurrying. You guys can come to the station later. After they checked out at the hospital. Or he can visit you guys there. Up to you."

Terrence came to stand by me. He closed his eyes for a

second before speaking. When he did, he was biting his lip. It looked like he was fighting back tears.

"He had them locked in the bathroom. Right outside the door was a roll of plastic sheeting and an electric saw like you'd use to cut a turkey."

I felt bile rise to my throat. We'd come just in time.

Terrence frowned as he examined my face for the first time since I'd come upstairs.

"Your face is bright red and your hair is...wet."

"I saw him," I said. "He sprayed me with mace or tear gas or something. I'm sorry. I tried to go after him, but I couldn't see shit. He was driving some small, dark car. That's all. Oh, he had brown hair."

"It doesn't matter. I got Gloria and Shalina back. That's all that counts."

Just then the small gathering at the apartment door parted, and his wife came out, holding their baby. The baby was smiling and cooing in her arms when she saw Terrence in front of her. Terrence raced over and hugged his wife, with the baby in between.

"They said you can drive me to the hospital. Just to check us out. I don't need to go in the ambulance," she said in a small voice.

"I don't have a car here, baby," Terrence said and turned to look at me. I took out my phone and dialed my driver buddy, Tony. He said he'd be there in ten.

His wife looked at me with a curious but calm expression.

"This is Gia," Terrence said. "The woman I told you about."

She smiled. "Nice to meet you."

I gave a slight nod. "My buddy Tony is going to be out front in a few minutes. He'll take you guys to the hospital. But I need to go after the man who kidnapped you. What can you tell me about him?"

In the elevator on the way down to the street, she told me what little she knew. The man had spoken very little. He'd kept her blindfolded until she was in the apartment's bathroom. He usually wore black slacks and a white shirt with shiny black shoes. He had wire-rimmed glasses and medium-brown hair cut short. When I asked her, she said he didn't really have any distinctive features. He looked like an average, white businessman.

I thought about that. Yeah. Made sense. A hide-in-plain-sight sort of assassin. The scariest kind.

"So no moles or scars? No weird facial tics or oddities of speech?"

She sighed. "No."

I thought harder. "What did he say to you that you can remember?"

She swallowed, suddenly seeming nervous.

"You okay, baby?" Terrence asked.

She thrust her shoulders back. "Yes. I opened the door, thinking it was Terrence." She gave him a quick glance. He nodded encouragingly. "He slammed it in hard and knocked me down. I cut my arm. He had Shalina before I could stand up."

Just as I'd suspected. At that point, she'd do anything he said.

"He took Shalina and told me to follow."

"That's the first time he spoke?"

"Yes. He said, 'Come with me. If you do what I say, I won't kill your baby.'"

I could see tears forming in the corners of her eyes.

"I had to go," she said.

"Of course you did," I said. "Anyone would have." I thought of Rosalie and how caring about her had made me more vulnerable. She was my Achilles heel.

"He told me to get in the backseat and then gave me Shalina. I tried to open the door, but the child lock was on. He made me put on a blindfold that was on the seat. He only let me take off the blindfold once we were in the bathroom."

"Is there anything else he said? Was that it?"

She nodded.

I realized I'd only asked what he'd said to her.

"Did you hear anything else? In the rest of the apartment."

She looked off in the distance as if she was thinking.

"It's fine. You can call me later if something comes back to you." I turned to go.

"Wait. I did hear something."

She said she'd pressed her face on the ground so she could see under the slight crack under the bathroom door. She'd watched his polished black shoes pace the floor. Then she heard a small sound. He was speaking to someone on the phone. "I have them," he had said.

There was silence for a few seconds, she said, but then the man spoke again, saying something about a "fifth target."

She closed her eyes for a second. I wondered if she'd seen the roll of plastic and the electric knife.

"Anything else?"

"Before Terrence came, I heard him shouting. He was swearing and banging around. He said something about night falling."

Night Fall.

As Tony pulled up, I turned to Terrence. "Where are you going after the hospital? If he has a hit on you, he's not just going to go away."

"I'm going up to Oregon. I got a cousin up there. We're just going to stop and get my car at Danny's and then we'll leave."

"Don't even go home to pack," I said.

His wife's eyes met mine "We won't. We're not taking any more chances."

I'D JUST PULLED onto my street, ready to have it out with James. I'd steeled myself to confront whatever bullshit was there between us. I'd just taken off my bike helmet when my phone pinged. It was a text from Danny.

He'd found another address connected to The Cleaner.

I put my helmet back on.

I'd deal with James later.

38

He watched the dark-haired woman and Hall and his family exit the building from his hideout in the building across the street—a third-floor office he'd broken into. He had been waiting a long time. It felt like hours. He wished he had his rifle and scope. He could take out Terrence Hall from here and be gone before the police made it down from the fourth floor.

What he couldn't figure out was who the dark-haired woman was. He tilted his head, thinking and watching her. She had long hair and wore jeans and boots and a motorcycle jacket.

When he'd come out of the back door, he'd sprayed the mace but hadn't been certain what or who he was dealing with. Until he saw her crumple and spotted the gun, he'd figured her for another resident of the building who'd been in the wrong place at the wrong time.

He lifted his phone and took a picture of her. When he got back online, he'd message MagnusOpus and The Patriot the picture. "Who the fuck is this Jessica Jones character?" he'd ask.

Two EMTs exited the building and got into the ambulance that was double parked in front of the building. A few seconds later, he watched as the dark-haired woman ushered the small family into a car that pulled up. When it left, she walked over to a motorcycle, strapping on a helmet and scattering gravel as she sped away. He watched, waiting for the police to leave.

When they walked out, they only had a small evidence bag. He knew they wouldn't find much. He'd kept the rental apartment safe house bare bones other than the laptop he'd stuck in his bugout bag. It was burned anyway. Once they got into their squads and pulled away, he finally left.

Back at his house in San Mateo, he pulled into the garage and waited for the door to close before he got out of his car. He immediately logged onto a spare laptop he had retrieved from a closet and checked all the footage on his security cameras. Nobody had disturbed the house while he'd been gone. Good. He was happy to be home. The rental was good for jobs in the city, but it never felt like home. Not like this place did. Midnight came up and purred, twirling around his ankles.

In the kitchen, he glanced over to make sure the cat's water and food dispenser had been working properly. Last thing he wanted was to come home to a dead kitty after a bad day.

Today was a bad day. He'd been made, despite all the precautions he had taken. That could not ever happen again. He would make sure of it.

He would punish himself by not eating. And by cleaning and washing and ironing all his clothes.

Yes, that would make him feel better. He ripped all his black pants and white dress shirts off their hangers and kicked them into a pile on the floor. He would wash them, dry them, and then iron every last shirt even if it took all night. Only then would he would be able to sleep.

Just as he was about to scoop up the clothes and take them to the laundry room, his phone buzzed on the dresser. It was lying neatly between a row of brand new deodorant sticks on one side and a half dozen bottles of aftershave lined up on the other.

Nobody would ever say he smelled bad. Not like when he was in middle school. That would never happen again.

A dark flash of memory raced into his consciousness. A stab of fury and humiliation accompanied it as he flashed back to a moment in the boy's locker room where all the other boys were holding their noses and making exaggerated gagging sounds as they walked past him and his locker. One dickhead jock even shoved him into the steel locker as he passed and then said, "Oh fuck. Now I'm going to smell like dog ass from brushing up against him. Disgusting."

After they left, with his heart racing, he'd sniffed under his armpits, but they didn't really smell bad, which worried him more than anything—was he used to smelling bad, or could he just not smell himself?

The phone buzzed again, jolting him out of his dark reverie.

His heart pounded as he glanced down. The text was from MagnusOpus.

"Stay off the Night Fall website. You're done there for now. But you've still got two more contracts to execute. Hold off on ShadowKing. Storm is back in town."

Within seconds, he'd grabbed his laptop and his large weapons suitcase from under the bed and was out the door.

39

THE NIGHT AIR FELT CRISP AND COOL AS I ZIPPED SOUTH DOWN THE mostly deserted freeway on my Blackbird, heading to the San Mateo address Danny had given me. Off to my right there was still the slightest pink of twilight in the sky. The air was crisp and carried the salty scent of the sea. On the straightaways, when there were no other vehicles around, I let my Blackbird rip. She was my second Blackbird. My first one was fast, but I wanted even faster, so I found a 2007 Honda CBR1100XX Super Blackbird in immaculate condition. I'd paid dearly for her because she was considered one of the fastest motorcycles in the world. She supposedly topped out at 178.5 miles per hour, but I'd only taken her to 140.

I wanted fast—not to show off or for the adrenaline rush—but in case a lot depended on it. I didn't want a lack of horsepower to cost me my life. It nearly had in the past.

Tonight, though, I took her to 120 for the sheer pleasure of it. It also helped me squash the anxiety in the pit of my belly. I'd texted James at a stoplight, telling him I would be even later than I'd thought. He ignored my text.

Before long, the exit for San Mateo appeared.

My bike was not quiet, so I decided to park three houses early. Taking my gun out, I walked the rest of the way, keeping an eye on the windows I passed. If the assassin had come straight here from the apartment, he'd be there now.

I paused in front of the house. It was small. A bungalow, really, with tidy landscaping, a freshly mowed lawn, and a few hedges. Nothing fancy, but clean and neat.

Drapes covered the large picture window. From out front, it looked like all the lights were off. It was too early for him to be in bed. But maybe I could peek into the house from the backside.

I crept to the side of the house. There was one small window with block glass. A bathroom probably. A small, waist-high metal gate led to the backyard. I poked my head around the corner of the house. A small patio contained a café table and two chairs. A tiny patch of lawn there was also neatly mowed. A back door with an upper pane of glass led to the patio.

I opened the gate. It didn't squeak. Holding my gun, I made my way to the window, keeping my body pressed against the house. I very slowly turned my head to look in the window with one eye. A light was on over the stove, but the house seemed deserted. I'd take my chances.

I slipped out of my leather jacket and put my fist inside it before punching out a small pane of glass near the door handle. I reached in and undid the lock, keeping my eyes on the hallway leading out of the kitchen. At the sound of breaking glass, a hairless cat had skittered away, limping oddly.

Leading with my gun, I stepped into the kitchen and immediately pressed myself against the wall to one side of the entryway to the rest of the house. I held my breath, heart pounding, ears straining.

When I didn't hear anything, I poked my head around the corner. A small lamp was on in the living room. Keeping my back to the wall, I crept inside, scanning the room. It took about five minutes for me to clear the whole house, including the closets and under the beds.

I went back into the kitchen. My eyes immediately focused on a glass on the small table. I reached over and felt it. Still cold. I lifted it to my nose. Grapefruit juice.

I'd just missed him. He must've been warned. Again.

Feeling a little more confident I was alone, I did another walkthrough of the house.

The living room was Spartan except for a giant cat gymnastic type thing made of rug remnants. The end table had a framed picture of the cat I'd seen earlier. A small basket contained cat toys.

In the bedroom, there was a miniature metal bed with a leopard print cushion. For the damn cat. Another container had more cat toys. Crazy cat guy for sure.

In the bedroom, there was surefire proof he'd left in a hurry. The house was excruciatingly tidy and neat, so the huge pile of clothes on the floor outside the closet seemed out of place.

I kicked at them a little with my foot to see if there was anything underneath. I felt something, so I reached down and began shuffling through the pile. It was only a pair of shoes. I looked in the closet again. It was empty.

I went back to the clothes, holding them up one-by-one to confirm my theory. Yes. The white shirts were identical. The black pants, all the same.

The cat came up to me then, purring and rubbing against my legs. It had a small bandage on one leg.

"Hey, princess. Aren't you a spoiled one?"

I reached down to scratch behind its ears briefly before I headed toward the dresser. And searched every drawer. A platform bed had white sheets, a white comforter, and white pillowcases on it. A charger was plugged in next to a lamp on the right side of the double bed. An oak dresser only contained items in the top two drawers. White underwear neatly rolled in the top one. Black socks neatly rolled in the lower.

In the bathroom, the medicine cabinet contained generic toiletries. There was not one single thing in the house that gave any indication of who this guy was. It was as impersonal as a hotel room. No pictures. No personal belongings. Creepy. The only thing that made me believe this guy had a pulse was the cat.

In the living room was a small desk with a charger cord stuck to one side. This is where he must plug in his laptop. What I wouldn't give to hand *that* over to Danny and his hacker friends.

The refrigerator was empty except for a few cans of grapefruit juice and two dozen stacks of fancy canned cat food. I checked the trash under the sink. It contained some boxes from frozen dinners. Healthy, heart-smart ones. So the guy did eat. I peeked in the freezer. Yep. Same ones. Only two varieties though. Like his clothes. Nothing conspicuous or different. This guy obviously didn't like variety, did he?

I wondered how I could use that against him. That's when I noticed something odd on the kitchen counter. As soon as I realized what it was, I pretended not to see it, picking up the cat and stroking it as I continued surveying the house.

40

CARL FINALLY MESSAGED BLAKE BACK.

"Sorry. Trying to deal with a small problem."

"Me too. A big flipping problem," Blake wrote. "The hitter—the one that *the Patriot, the gosh darn police chief,* hired—messaged me. He's been made. We are so screwed."

Carl took a full minute to respond.

"We're not screwed. I've deleted everything to do with the hitter on Night Fall. The posts but also all the backend stuff that most people can't see. There is no way anybody can trace him to you. No way. I've been in touch with him. What I can't figure out is how he knew that Night Fall had hired him. Do you think the chief told him? That's not cool. How did he know it was us?"

"YOU TELL ME!" Blake wrote in all caps. He was furious. Carl was head of security. This was an utter disaster.

Carl didn't respond. Blake steeled himself not to write anything until Carl responded. When a minute had passed, Blake dropped to the ground and started doing pushups. Anything to stop him from replying first.

After fifty-eight pushups, he saw Carl had responded.

"He's not going to give us up," Carl wrote back. "He has a

reputation to uphold. If he ever wants to work as a hitter again, he'll keep his fucking mouth shut about Night Fall. He's a pro."

"Big deal," Blake wrote. "He could fleece us of every penny for the rest of our lives, threatening to expose me."

"Nah," Carl wrote. "He's an addict."

"Even worse."

"Not drugs, dude. He's addicted to killing. His entire identity is wrapped up in being a hit man for hire. Check this out."

A link appeared.

Blake clicked on it. It was the hitter's website.

The website featured a white circle surrounded by black with hash marks like a paper target at a shooting range and a figure of a man holding a gun centered in the bullseye.

It was a lot like a frame from an old James Bond movie trailer. There was a single splotch of red on the target's chest.

Blake clicked on the red since there was nothing else on the page. He was taken into a screen that showed testimonial after testimonial attesting to the hitter's discretion and talent. There were about thirty. Some included their location: Hong Kong. None of them had names attached, but a few of them had pictures and descriptions of the victims. Those had an asterisk. Blake scrolled down to the bottom of the page to read the description attached to the asterisk. It said, "Details shared after approval by contractor."

"What's your point?" Blake wrote to Carl. For some reason, Blake felt a flicker or suspicion against Carl. He'd always trusted his high school friend. But now he was wondering if Carl had communicated directly with the hitter. He sure seemed to know a lot about the guy.

"He's discreet," Carl wrote. "His business depends on it."

"Okay," he wrote to Carl. "What now?"

"You need to reach out to The Patriot. Let him know what's

going on. He might have his own ideas to deal with The Cleaner."

Blake really liked the sound of that.

"K," he typed.

"Feel better?" Carl wrote.

"Some."

"Good. I need to talk to you about that other problem."

"What now?"

"My fed contact says that there is a multi-jurisdictional task force ready to move on you tomorrow."

41

SITTING IN HIS CAR PARKED ON A STREET THRIVING WITH CAFES and restaurants, the Cleaner logged onto his spare laptop using a national coffee chain's WIFI and watched the footage of the woman pilfering his house hours earlier.

She'd never noticed the small surveillance camera on the kitchen counter next to his toaster. It looked like a stereo speaker. He watched her go through his things, and his stomach churned. She had contaminated everything.

He held his breath as she came closer to the camera. She leaned over and scribbled on a notepad he had neatly set out. Then she folded the paper and set it on his kitchen table before she moved into the bedroom. Another camera on his bedroom clock recorded her movements in there. He felt like he was going to vomit as he watched her rifle through his clothing. But when she pet his cat, he closed his eyes. No, not the cat. Not Midnight.

It was right then and there that he decided he would kill the woman for free. Just for contaminating his life.

He sent MagnusOpus a picture of the dark-haired woman. The response had been immediate. "Find out who she is. She's a loose end. She needs to be dealt with. Hold off on killing Storm.

Use her as bait. For the woman. And don't contact Vlad again. He has enough to worry about. I'm your main contact now."

Bait? The Cleaner smiled. It would be his pleasure.

He slammed the laptop closed. First, he'd grab the note the dark-haired woman left to see if it could lead him to her. And Midnight. He'd rescue his cat from starvation. That bitch had dumped the cat's food in the toilet. He started his car and headed toward San Mateo.

Once on his street, he cautiously approached the house, but there was no sign of anyone staking it out or spying on it, so he parked and went in the back way. That bitch had broken the window.

Once inside, he grabbed Midnight and the note the woman had left for him, and ran back outside, keeping to the shadows. Everything in his once beloved home was contaminated now. He wouldn't be able to tell what she touched and what she hadn't.

As he drove away, the white slip of paper lay unread on the passenger seat. It was as if the note was glowing. He would read it when he was back safe in the storage locker.

He would search every word for clues. He would study her words and her picture until he knew how he could find her.

He was now homeless and it was her fault.

He would make her pay.

But first he had a little stop to make.

The banging in his trunk was getting annoying. He glanced over to make sure his torture kit was still in the backseat. He wondered how far he'd have to go before the girl gave up the bitcoin she'd taken.

Not very far, he guessed.

As he pulled into the storage shed lot, he rolled down his window and gave a jaunty wave to the man in the office, who recognized him and waved him on him.

He turned the music up as he passed, just in case.

The sounds of Exodus poured out, drowning out any noise that might come from the trunk. He sang along and pounded the steering wheel to the beat. He hadn't tortured anyone for a while. He hoped she was stubborn and didn't easily reveal where she'd hidden the bitcoin. He hoped the proceedings were long and drawn out.

He wanted this night to last.

42

On my way home from the assassin's house, Darling called me.

I'd planned on going home before dawn and sneaking into bed before James woke for the day. That changed with her call.

"Bad news. The apartment manager at Charlie's place said he saw the girl go into her apartment earlier tonight. An hour later, he knocked to give condolences about her mom. Door was cracked, place ransacked. No Charlie."

He got her. Shit.

"I'm going to take it as a good sign that the manager didn't find her body."

"We also got word that the feds are coming to town."

"The bad ones or good ones," I said.

"The legit ones. They want to take Night Fall's founder down. Supposed to happen tomorrow morning."

"That's a good thing, right?" I asked.

"It's good unless they think this is an excuse to kill Charlie before she returns their money. There's no doubt that they already know about the raid. They might consider her a dangerous loose end. What she knows could put the website founder away for life."

"I'll head to Danny's."

———

"THEY GOT HER. I HEARD," he said as soon as I walked in.

"Oh, Danny," I said. "I'm so sorry. Charlie must've become worried when she couldn't reach her mom and came home."

"I met her once. Her mom. At a school thing. She was volunteering. She was really nice."

"I'm sorry," I said again.

He changed the subject.

"I got some more info on our guy. He's smart. For a hitter."

"A hitter?"

Danny glanced over at me. "A hit man. Usually they are kind of dumb, more brawn than brains. This guy seems different."

I pulled up a chair at his table full of computers.

"In what way?"

The hit man was using a computer with zero personal information on it, Danny said. It seemed to be primarily a port to access the dark web. Even so, Danny had been able to dig up the hit man's search history for the past week. As soon as Danny had snuck in the back door to the assassin's computer, he'd starting copying files. Even after the guy started shutting things down and deleting items, Danny was still copying things in real time.

"I think I got most of what he was trying to ditch," Danny said. "He spends a lot of time on the dark web. Not only Night Fall but also his own site. I was able to access several usernames he has. Those usernames haven't been looking for work, so to speak, for the past three weeks, so we can assume he got hired to do these hits around then. With that said, we can trace the history of the job postings there."

"They keep the posts up?"

"Nope. They're deleted. But they leave shadows for those of us who know how to find them. Like when you write on a pad of paper and rip the page you've written on off the pad. There remains a faint copy. That's what I was able to find."

"You got the original assignment? The hits?"

"Yes."

"Did you find out who posted the job?"

"Yes." He couldn't hide his grin.

"Let me have it."

"He goes by MagnusOpus. But he did it through another guy called The Patriot."

"Who? What? Where? Give me some context, sailor."

"MagnusOpus is Vlad's right-hand man."

"You lost me."

"Vlad is the guy who founded the Night Fall website."

"Got it. So who is The Patriot? The killer?

"We'll get to that," Danny said and gave me a grin I'd never seen before. "This is another room in Night Fall—one that is only accessible through invitation. The other hitter site mentioned it, but it was really low-key, unobvious. At first, I didn't pay any attention to it. I actually thought it was a video game, but it's real.

The page had a banner that said, "Hit Men for Hire."

"Not very subtle."

He pointed to a post with 1,000 comments. The post said, "Is this site legit? Can I really arrange a hit on my wife?"

Danny scrolled down to a post marked "Admin."

It said, "Why would we answer that question without a show of faith. You know what to do."

The commenter underneath said, "In other words, pay up, and you'll find out."

Several posters had replied that they'd either heard of

someone or knew someone who'd paid for a hit on this site, and they had been fulfilled. An equal number of commenters said the opposite—that the website just took their money. Or worse, that after ordering a hit, the buyer had been arrested.

I looked up at Danny. "Seems like a joke to me. A scam."

"It's a double-cross blind."

"English."

"Both sets of commenters are right."

"Explain."

"I did a little digging around. Here's the real story. You can, in fact, hire a legitimate hit man through this site. There are 400 registered, legit, assassins-for-hire on this website. If someone orders a hit, follows the rules, and pays, it's a smooth transaction.

"However, if someone is fucking around and doesn't pay or screws up, the website forwards all their information to the police."

He paused and raised an eyebrow.

I wasn't in the mood to play games. "Keep talking."

"So the FBI and cops believe this website is run by a bunch of anti-criminal hackers who are helping *them* out."

"How stupid can they be?"

"Right?" Danny said. "Because at the same time, Night Fall is flourishing as a middleman, actually connecting hit men with customers."

"How is this connected to our assassin?"

"There's a thread. It's in code and was deleted earlier today, but I got it thanks to our killer's files. In it, it's pretty clear they're talking about murder for hire. There are three people on this thread—Night Fall's right-hand man, MagnusOpus, the assassin, who goes by The leaner, and the middle man, The Patriot, who Night Fall hired to deal with the assassin." Danny paused dramatically and raised an eyebrow. "The Patriot? Well, let's just say they hired a middle man who was, let's say, above the law."

My heart started to race. My eyes widened.

"Don't fuck with me, Danny."

He just smiled and nodded.

I screamed with excitement and grabbed him in a big hug. He pulled back and his face was tomato red. "Sorry." I said, but couldn't stop grinning. "Can we prove it?"

My blood was pumping. *Holy shit.*

"You have proof of this?" I asked again. "Something that would stand up in a court of law? Something that would allow authorities to take him down? For real? For good?"

"Yes. Right here." He tapped a screen.

"There?"

"I've sent it to some good friends of mine. Told them that if anything happens to me, or if they don't hear back from me by this time tomorrow night, to get it to the people I've listed."

I froze. "What are you talking about Danny?"

He swallowed. His Adam's apple bobbed in his large, pale neck.

"As soon as I got the info, I got an anonymous message on a super-deep website group I'm part of."

"What did it say, Danny?"

"It said, the police chief knew I was on to him. To watch my back."

"Oh fuck. *Fuck.*" I looked around wildly. "Why can't we send that file to the Department of Justice right now? If we also send it to every newspaper in the country, they can't all bury it—even if there *is* someone in the DOJ or FBI or CIA protecting the chief. If the media gets hold of this... I mean, I don't understand why we're waiting."

He closed his eyes for a brief second. I knew why we were waiting. Storm.

"Danny, please think about what you are doing."

"I'm playing a different game, Gia."

I froze. Danny had never looked more certain or more confident in his life. He held his head high, and his shoulders were back as he said, "I sent a message to the chief—as The Patriot. I told him if he arranged to let Charlie go, I wouldn't send the file that revealed everything—who he was and how he had paid a hitman to kill four San Francisco residents. I told him that he needed to get ahold of his dark web buddies and tell them to back off. To let Charlie go."

It was only after he spoke that he looked down, refusing to hold my gaze.

Danny knew as well as I did that James and I had spent the past year trying to prove the chief was a crooked motherfucker, and he was prepared to bury that proof to save Charlie. I closed my eyes for a second.

"I'm sorry, Gia," he said.

I opened my eyes and gave him a small smile, squeezing his arm. "You did the right thing. Her life is more important than..."

I couldn't finish the sentence. I didn't know how I was going to tell James. Making the chief pay, legally, was all James lived for. Me? I'd rather have the chief die a slow, painful death. Well, at least that's what I told myself. But what got James out of bed every morning was the thought of that day being the day that the chief would be arrested and sent to prison for the rest of his life.

But a girl's life was at stake. A girl who was now an orphan like me. A girl that Danny cared about.

"You did the right thing," I repeated. And I meant it. But the words had cost me a lot.

I could see Danny's shoulders visibly relax. "I know—"

"You need to get out of here," I said, interrupting him. "They're probably heading here right now. If they kill you, they

don't have to worry about whatever it is you threatened to do—
to get the information out."

"It's called doxing."

I opened my mouth to say I didn't care what it was called,
but then I simply said, "You need to leave. With me. Now."

He stood and crossed his arms. "I'm not going anywhere,
Gia."

Oh my God. Not another one. First Terrence, then Danny.

"Yes you are!" I knew I sounded like a shrill mother, and I
didn't care. "Please, Danny. Those fuckers are murderers. Police
who kill. The chief will use everything in his power to make sure
you don't share that information. You are in danger. Look what
they did to James!"

"I'm not leaving."

He stood there in front of me with his arms crossed like a big
fucking semi-truck that I couldn't budge if my life depended on
it. I can't remember the last time I was so angry.

I glared at him and crossed my own arms. "Well, then
neither am I."

He deflated just a little. Barely enough to notice if you
weren't paying attention.

"Gia..." His voice was pleading.

"Danny, I brought this shitshow on you. I brought you into it.
I'm not walking away and letting them...letting them...." I
stopped, realizing that there was nothing I could say or do. He'd
made up his mind.

He turned his back on me and began fiddling with his drone.

"Let's start surveillance."

Within a few minutes, he'd sent the drone out the window
and was sitting in front of his bank of computers watching the
camera feed.

I leaned over his shoulder. "There," I pointed. "What's that
black car?"

"That's my neighbor, Rick. He's an Uber driver."

"Okay, what about that guy standing next to the building."

"Manuel. He's having a smoke break. He works right around the corner at Smart Stop."

After a while I grew bored watching the drone footage.

"This is all we're going to do?" I said. "Just wait for them to come try to kill you?"

"It's not like we can call the police, can we?" he said.

I frowned.

"I've got an idea," I said. "Can you get into the assassin's computer again?"

Danny nodded, his eyes narrowing. "The one I hacked is done. But if he logs onto any computer with his old usernames and passwords, I've got him. And believe me, he will. If not right away, then soon."

43

BLAKE STARED AT THE MESSAGE FROM CARL. IT TOOK A MINUTE for him to comprehend:

"I got bad news. I know who stole your bitcoin and he's ready to destroy everything. We're royally fucked, dude," MagnusOpus had written.

Blake was confused. *He?* Carl had claimed Storm had taken the bitcoin. And now he's saying it's someone else? A he.

"Who?" Blake typed.

"Some kid who lives in the Tenderloin. He just threatened the police chief. Says he has a file that will dox us all. If we don't let Storm go, he's going to the DOJ.

"He says he's got everything on us. Everything. He hacked in and somehow got all the shit I deleted. He's got proof that me, you, and the chief are connected to The Cleaner. He knows everything. Probably even our real names and identities. But it gets worse."

The cursor blinked. Blake was about to punch the monitor. *What? What is worse than that?*

Finally, the message appeared. "The chief contacted me and is playing hard ball. He says if we don't take out the kid, he's pulling all protection, going to tell all. Unless we shut the kid down, all bets are off. The chief will turn on us. It's time to pull the plug, my friend, and get out. I hope you have an escape plan."

"What about the bitcoin?" Blake wrote. "Storm took millions from us."

"At this point, It's not worth it, dude. Let it go."

"Where's the hitter?"

"He's busy with Charlie."

Blake thought about that for a second. He had to make a choice. The bitcoin or his life.

He'd been reading books about successful entrepreneurs. The book he'd read this afternoon talked about how leaders know when to pivot. This was one of those moments.

"Tell the Cleaner to drop everything *immediately* and head to the Tenderloin."

44

After sharing my idea, I also told Danny that the FBI was going to take Night Fall down in the morning.

"Darling said we need to find Charlie by morning, or any leverage we might have goes up in smoke."

We hadn't heard or seen anyone come near Danny's building, and he still refused to leave.

Then I told him my plan. He finally agreed to my idea when he realized it meant I would leave his apartment.

"You threatened them and told them if they didn't release Charlie you'd turn over the files, right?"

"Yes."

"But we haven't made a plan for the exchange."

He frowned. "No."

"Let's do it then."

Danny slid aside a small, metal security plate from in front of the laptop's camera. I was sitting in front of the camera. "Go," Danny said.

"We haven't heard from you. And we are getting tired of waiting," I said. "We need proof that she's alive. I've taken over your screen. I can see anything you put there. I'll give you two minutes to give me that proof or we hit send."

I watched my message appear in real time on the assassin's monitor as I typed.

I sat back, holding my breath, afraid to glance to the side where Danny was. I stared at the assassin's screen. The backdrop was empty. There was not a single folder or document or image on the screen. It was black.

Two minutes later, I saw a cursor hopping around and then a picture appeared on the black screen. It was Charlie. It was a movie file. It began to play. The pretty face I'd seen in her mother's photos was now ravaged with pain. Her face was streaked with black from her mascara running as she cried. Her sandy blonde hair hung dark and wet around her face. Her cat-eye glasses were gone. Her bloodshot eyes looked wildly around. Then the screen went black again.

Fuck. We needed to get to her right away.

I typed again.

"You know our demands already: Give us Charlie and we'll destroy the files we copied. But I need an address. Now. Your time is up."

I held my breath as I watched the black screen. After a few seconds, an address appeared. Then a still image appeared on the screen. It was of Charlie. Her face was scrunched up in pain as if she'd just been punched. Her bare arms were flecked with red, small cuts. A man stood behind her. The image only showed him from the neck down. He held a large, serrated knife in his gloved hands. The knife's edge had blood on it.

Danny slammed the laptop shut. "Motherfuck." He was typing angrily. Finally, he looked up. "Address is a storage locker facility in Potrero Hill."

"Can you send the drone to watch me?" I was suddenly nervous.

"You really think he'll give us Charlie?" Danny said. His voice was filled with anxiety.

"We're sort of out of other options."

He looked at me with desperation.

I reached over and grabbed my leather jacket. As I did my phone dinged. I looked down. It was a message from James. "Going to my mother's. Dropped Rosalie at the salon."

What the...?

But I was in a hurry. I needed to get to Charlie. I didn't even reply.

"Good luck," I said to Danny as I got ready to go. "Promise to take the secret passageway out of here if anyone shows up.

A door in his basement led to a series of tunnels that ran under the Tenderloin. There were several dead ends, but one led to a building near Darling's salon.

He didn't answer.

"Secret passageway. Right?" I repeated.

He sighed and rolled his eyes like a sullen teenager. "Right."

"Wish me luck, sailor," I said, trying to make him smile.

He scowled. "Just don't die, Gia."

45

It was almost too easy. He put the padlock on the storage space and drove back out the main entrance waving again casually at the guard. He didn't care if the guy saw his face. He was never coming back here again.

Right after the dark-haired woman had messaged him, he received another message from MagnusOpus. Night Fall had deposited more than two hundred bitcoin into his account. More than two million dollars. It was a down payment. MagnusOpus said a fake ID along with a ticket to Los Angeles would be waiting in a locker at the train station. Number seventy-six. From there, he'd catch a plane to anywhere he wanted to go.

But he had one last job to do.

They told him to forget about Charlie. There was a bigger threat. A kid in the Tenderloin who'd hacked his computer. He'd taken off immediately. He'd left the girl alive. Just in case the dark-haired woman had planned on keeping her word—the girl's life in exchange for her destroying the file that would expose them all.

Just in case.

Right now, he hoped none of that would matter. With a new

ID and the money Night Fall had promised, he could simply disappear.

He only had to do one thing before the ID was deposited in the locker. Kill the kid in the Tenderloin. MagnusOpus said he'd pay him another three million dollars in bitcoin when the job was done. Best money he'd made in his life. He would still crave his life as a hit man, but he could be more selective about which jobs he took.

Only one thing stood between him and this freedom. The kid.

46

THE DRONE'S SMALL, FLASHING LIGHT WAS SO HIGH UP IN THE SKY I could barely see it.

I was standing in the parking lot of the storage facility near my motorcycle, I could feel my Beretta Pico in my back waistband.

Satisfied that I was as ready as I'd ever be, I headed toward the office at the entrance to the driveway. I wasn't sure how stuff like this was handled. Was this Fort Knox-type security or just a way to prevent thieves from ransacking all the lockers? Would I have to make up a story to be let in? I'd try telling the truth first and see what happened. The guy at the desk was skinny with deep bags under his eyes and wrinkled hands. He had a paperback splayed in front of him.

"Hey," I said. "I'm meeting a friend inside. I won't be long."

I tried to act nonchalant as fuck.

"Locker number?"

"215."

"Think your friend just left."

The blood drained from my face. I was too late. "What?"

"Six foot one. 175 pounds. Short brown hair."

I leaned forward onto the desk. "Was he alone?"

"No clue, lady. I didn't search his car."

I exhaled. "I need access to the locker. Now. There might be a girl inside."

"What?" The guard's forehead crinkled. He wasn't computing.

"Now!"

He stood but still didn't seem to comprehend.

The drone was suddenly on my shoulder, or at least a few feet above me, making a quiet whirring sound.

"What the—?" the guard said.

"Hurry!" I didn't wait for him to answer. I followed the signs down the narrow road toward the low 200s. A padlock was on the garage door of 215. I pounded with both fists. "Charlie? Charlie if you're in there we're coming. We're here to help. Charlie?"

The drone was above me. I looked up at it with despair. Then I pressed my ear to the corrugated metal door. Nothing. This was bad.

The guard caught up to me. He fumbled with some keys and pulled up short.

"Hey," he said. "Padlocks aren't allowed!"

"Do something!" I shouted.

He turned and ran away.

I dialed 911. "There is a kidnap victim at the Golden Hour Storage Facility on 8700 Cleveland Street. We need police and an ambulance. Come quickly. It's a matter of life and death."

I hung up just as the guard returned, hefting some massive bolt cutters.

"Got just the thing," he said. He popped the padlock off, and we both reached down to pull the door up. As soon as it started to rise, I rolled under it, coming to a standing position with the flashlight of my phone on. Right in front of me, in the beam of light, I saw Charlie bound to a chair with thick strips of silver tape.

The poor thing was soaking wet. As I drew closer, I saw electrodes attached to her neck, her wrists and some wires leading into the neckline of her shirt. Her face was streaked with black from her mascara running down her face. She'd been crying. She also had small cuts down her arms. He'd been torturing her, just as I'd thought.

I raced over and ripped the gag out of her mouth. She gasped and sobbed.

"I don't have the bitcoin. I never did."

"I know honey, I know."

With a flick of my dagger, I freed her from the chair by cutting the twist ties binding her wrists and ankles.

She collapsed in my arms. I held her small wet body close. My heart pounded so loudly in my ears, I could barely hear anything else, but I clocked the sound of distant sirens. *Good.*

"He killed my mom." She buried her face in my shirt, sobbing.

"I'm so, so sorry."

I held her and rocked her until the EMTs rushed into the locker and took over. I handed her over to them and stood. I stepped outside to give the EMTs room to work. I looked up in the sky for the drone but didn't hear it or see it. When I looked down the road, I saw it smashed on the ground.

My heart leaped into my throat.

I knew where the assassin had gone.

47

As I ran to the parking lot, I ordered my phone to dial Danny. It went straight to voicemail. *Fuck me.*

"Call 911," I ordered my phone, breathing heavily as I ran.

"911? Where is your emergency?" the operator said.

I rattled off Danny's address and apartment number first. "There's a man with a gun. Please send the cops."

"Your name?" If I said Gia Santella, she might not help. From what Darling had told me, the chief had distributed my name and picture across town, saying I was a "5150." It was the penal code but also shorthand the cops used when dealing with a crazy person.

I hung up. I nearly laid my bike down when I hit a small patch of gravel in my hurry to get out of the parking lot. When I'd straightened out, I gunned it.

I wanted to dial Danny again, but I was going so fast I needed both hands on the handlebars to maintain control. I slowed as I passed Howard Street.

Last year, I'd attended the Oakland Day of the Dead celebration and stopped at one particularly beautiful ofrenda made in honor of a twenty-two-year-old black-haired beauty. The display contained her favorite foods and drinks and pictures. I stopped to talk to her father, who looked at me with his grief permanently etched on his face.

"She took the Howard exit too quickly and flipped her Jeep," he said. "I can just see her," he'd said wistfully. "She probably had her music blaring—maybe U2—and was happy and smiling and excited to meet her friends for a night of dancing. But she took the corner too fast."

He looked down.

"We all do such dumb things when we're young, not realizing that one simple mistake at the right time under the right circumstances can mean the end," he'd said.

I'd tried not to cry, listening to this man. I went home that night and thought about that girl for a very long time. I still think about her every single time I'm near Howard Street. How can I not?

I couldn't help but slow down because thinking of that dark-haired Mexican beauty had reminded me of Rosalie.

Having that little girl in my life meant I should be more careful. But I didn't want to. I really didn't want to let anyone else dictate my actions or my thoughts. I was torn. I didn't want to die, but I also knew I would risk my life to help people. Especially someone I loved, like Danny. I skidded to a stop in front of his building.

Miracle of miracles, a San Francisco P.D. squad car was already parked in front of the building. But the two cops sat in the squad like statues. I raced up and pounded on the window of the driver's side. The cop looked at his partner in the passenger seat. That officer reached for a clipboard, flipped through it, and then said something I couldn't hear through the closed window. I was about to blow a fucking gasket. They were wasting time.

"Why are you just sitting there?"

The cop in the driver's side rolled down his window while the other cop spoke on his cell phone, still peering down at the clipboard. The other cop said something into the phone and then nudged his partner. The window went up. The engine started. I looked over at the clipboard and saw my own face staring back at me. *Holy fucking shit.*

The chief had passed out my photo to the patrol officers. *What did it say*? I pounded on the window, but the squad pulled out, nearly running over my boot. *What the fuck*? The patrol vehicle simply left. I guess I was lucky they didn't arrest me.

I stood in the middle of the street, screaming for Danny and staring up at his window, which was dark. I'd never, ever seen it dark. Fear trickled across my scalp. Why hadn't I made him give me a key?

A head popped out of one of the first-floor windows. "Shut the fuck up! We're trying to sleep."

"Let me in! It's an emergency."

The man grumbled but pulled his head in. A few seconds later, I heard the door to the building click open. I raced over and upstairs to the fourth floor.

Danny's door was wide open. I'd expected to see a ransacked apartment, but all I saw was the controller for the drone on the floor by a chair.

He'd been taken by surprise. And it didn't appear that he'd put up a fight. I didn't understand. Unless...he'd managed to get away and made it to the secret passageway before the assassin arrived.

I ran outside the apartment and took the stairs two at a time to the basement. The door to the underground tunnel was open. *Thank God.*

The tunnel opened up into several other passageways. I could only assume that Danny had taken the one that led to the building near Darling's salon. A few of the tunnels led to dead ends, just walls of dirt. Another led to a metal gate, beyond which was a sheer drop that led to the sewer system.

I hoped Danny had a massive head start. He was a big guy and a far cry from a fitness buff. He spent probably twenty hours a day in front of his various computers and monitors. I think he reluctantly slept for a few hours in the afternoon simply because he couldn't keep his eyes open any longer. But he definitely didn't take time to work out.

This always worried me because supposedly sitting is the new smoking, but never more than it worried me now. Danny couldn't outrun even an out-of-shape assassin. And other than his sheer size, he didn't have any way to really fight back.

I stepped into the dark tunnel, shining my phone's flashlight ahead of me, hoping that when I found Danny he'd still be alive.

48

HE DIDN'T LIKE RUNNING BLIND IN THE DIM LIGHT, SO HE WALKED quickly, keeping one palm stretched out in front of him. The tunnel had very dim, very old light bulbs strung every twenty feet or so. He could see a few feet in front of him but not very well. His other hand clutched his Ontario Marine Bayonet with the blade flat against his leg, poised to attack.

When he'd first stepped into the tunnel, he heard footsteps and heavy breathing, but he could no longer hear anything except the eerie drip of water coming from somewhere ahead.

He crept forward, listening intently.

It was only a matter of time.

He pushed back the doubt crowding his mind.

It was still nearly unfathomable that the kid had escaped him in the first place.

He'd underestimated his target. He'd assumed he could use the element of surprise to walk in and take him out silently and quickly. He didn't expect the kid to be waiting as soon as he stepped out of the stairwell.

The huge redheaded kid had swung something down on his head. He'd slumped to the ground, a black circle closing in on his vision. He'd fought against the searing pain and the desire to close his eyes and curl up into the fetal position. He had to stay alert and awake. He scrambled to his feet. By the time he had, the kid was gone down the stairs.

When he'd gotten back to the first floor, the kid had disappeared, but his heavy breathing a floor below had given him away. He'd heard the slightest click of a door closing and then silence.

He took the next flight of stairs to the basement. There were three doors. He tried one, locked. He tired another, a storage closet. The third led to a yawning, black opening. He stepped inside. Soon, the light from the basement disappeared, and he was in darkness. He paused to listen, poised to duck, ready to attack, prepared to drop to the ground to avoid another unforeseen attack.

The only reason the kid had escaped him in the first place was because he'd underestimated him. Stupid, rookie move.

It wouldn't happen again.

Moving forward in the dim tunnel, he strained to hear anything—any little noise that would indicate where the target was.

Then he heard it. The tiniest little sound. A whimper.

Not too far ahead. His adrenaline spiked. The last light was twenty feet back. He crept forward in the darkness.

It wouldn't be long now.

He pressed his back against the wall and slid forward inch by inch toward where he'd heard the sound. He kept his arm extended, stretching it along the wall in front of him. The wall disappeared. Quickly, he drew his hand back. An alcove or an entrance to another tunnel. He stopped his minute shuffling and held his breath, ears straining.

He was ninety-nine percent sure the kid was hiding in the

alcove, either waiting for him to pass so he could run the other way or waiting to attack him again.

His hand tensed on the knife at his side. He regulated his breathing, inhaling silently but deeply and slowly. He was like a coiled snake ready to strike. Like a spider waiting for the fly to crawl into his web.

He would wait for as long as it took.

Minutes passed, agonizingly slow, where the only sound he could distinguish was the sound of his own blood rushing in his ears. The quiet was starting to fuck with him when he heard it.

A soft, nearly inaudible sigh.

He extended the knife in front of him and took one step, squaring his body in front of the doorway. Before he could strike, he heard another sound. He froze.

A door had just opened somewhere.

49

DANNY SENSED THE MAN RIGHT OUTSIDE THE ALCOVE. HIS ARMS were about to fall off from holding the baseball bat above his head. With his night vision glasses, he'd clearly seen the man's palm glowing for a second before it had withdrawn.

If he weren't such a darn coward, he'd step out of the doorway and attack. But it had taken everything out of him to hit the man when he'd stepped out of the stairwell. The only thing that had enabled him to go through with it was knowing that he had killed Charlie's mother and maybe Charlie too.

He'd been controlling his drone, watching Gia at the entrance to the storage shed, when he'd heard his homeless friend, Jimmy, whistle. The special whistle of warning. The sharp, piercing one they'd agreed on that meant, *Get the fuck out now!*

He'd dropped the controls to the drone and only had time to grab a baseball bat as he ran for the stairwell. He opened the door but could already hear pounding footsteps on the floor below. Quietly, he closed the door, heart pounding and stood off to one side. Sweat poured down his face as the footsteps grew closer. He'd held the baseball bat above his head, his eyes closed. For a second his resolve wavered. He'd never hurt anyone in his life. He was a pacifist for crying out loud.

As the door to the stairwell opened, he remembered Charlie's mother. His eyes popped open, and he tightened the grip on the baseball bat. It only took three seconds for him to confirm that yes, this was a bad guy. This was The Cleaner. He wasn't a resident of the apartment. Danny swung the bat, and it glanced off the guy's head. He slumped to the ground, and Danny hoped with all his heart the guy was just knocked out. But he didn't wait around to find out.

He stepped over The Cleaner's body and took the stairs two at a time to the basement passageway. It was dim inside the tunnel but the few bulbs every fifteen feet or so made it possible to see a few feet in front of him. He ran, his heart pounding madly in his chest. He vaguely wondered if he could have a heart attack from the fright and exertion.

A few seconds later, he came to the split. He had a choice of three directions. His mind went utterly blank. He didn't know which way led to the opening near Gia's building. He couldn't remember even though his life might depend on his choice. He couldn't remember. He realized with horror that his life might well depend on remembering that one crucial bit of information. It seemed that the tunnel to the left would be the correct one because Gia's loft was to the left of his building. But he had no idea how much the tunnel twisted and turned.

He was still frozen with indecision when he heard a door open behind him followed by footsteps soon after, growing closer. The Cleaner was alive and coming after him. He picked the middle tunnel and ran, breathing heavily. It didn't take long to realize he had chosen wrong.

This was the tunnel that ended at the drop to the sewer. He ran to the gate and grabbed the bars, shaking them helplessly. The gate wouldn't budge. It didn't matter anyway because the gate wouldn't budge. He whirled and saw the small alcove. He gave a whimper of relief. He ducked into the alcove, pressing himself as tightly against the earth behind him as he could. He listened but could no longer hear footsteps. He managed to get a grip on his panting and listened more intently.

Soon he heard the slightest sound. The hitman *was* coming this way. He very slowly lifted the baseball bat above his head.

He waited until the muscles in his arms were trembling with fatigue from holding the bat. That had been when he saw the palm in front of the alcove. He steeled himself to step out and attack the son of a bitch who'd killed Charlie's mom. But he was paralyzed with fear. He wasn't sure what he was more afraid of —his own death or killing another human being.

He waited longer and then the man stepped right in front of him.

"Go time!" he thought, unsure where the words in his head had come from.

A banshee cry rose in his throat as he lunged forward, but the assassin had turned his head to look behind him and managed to step out of the way just in time. The baseball bat sliced through the air and struck the ground. His unchecked forward momentum caused him to fall face-first to the ground. He tasted dirt and was struggling to rise when he heard a familiar voice.

"Danny!" The shout fell somewhere between a command and a rallying cry. His entire body relaxed as he heard it. It would be okay now. Gia was here.

50

THE WOMAN WITH THE DARK HAIR. HE RECOGNIZED HER VOICE AS soon as it echoed down the tunnel.

How had she found him? She should've been at the storage shed wondering where he'd gone and rescuing that girl she was so worried about. She was smarter than he'd thought. He heard the pounding of footsteps and before he could react, she was there and on him, kicking at him like Bruce Fucking Lee. The first kick into his chest sent him flying. He thudded into that big lug of a kid's broad chest and practically bounced off back toward the girl. It threw her off enough for him to land a punch right in her eye socket.

He wasn't a very good close-combat fighter. His skills lay mainly in blending in, creeping up, and then killing someone with a weapon. He'd seen a pipe on the ground on the way in and should've grabbed it. The only weapon he still had on him was a small knife that slid into his belt buckle. It was more like a letter opener than a real knife, but it would work. He ducked down quickly and slashed at her leg with the blade, hoping to slice through her Achilles tendon and disable her. But the blade just skimmed across thick, leather boots.

While he was down there, he got a knee to the face, which sent him reeling back. He dropped to the floor and rolled, allowing him to avoid her ferocious stomping aimed at his head and throat.

He rolled against the wall and pushed himself back into a crouch as she headed his way. He lunged and slashed at her upper thigh with the blade. She bent over, and he raised the knife to slash at her face. Before he could, the kid brought the baseball bat down on his wrist. He heard bone shatter and he screamed. His knife went flying. Using his other hand, he brought the side of his palm up and backhanded the woman's head at her ear. She was taken off guard and went reeling. He heard the big kid yell and grunt behind him, and he ducked just as a powerful ham-sized fist whizzed through the air beside him. Before the woman could get back to her feet, he was up and running down the passageway.

51

"GIA? GIA? GIA?"

The words seemed to come from a long way away.

I was violently hoisted up and set on my feet like I was a rag doll being propped up. I blinked in the dark. In the dim light, I saw Danny's face right in front of mine.

"Gia? Are you okay? He's getting away."

It all came back. My head cleared, and I turned to run after the assassin.

I rounded a corner and saw him in front of me, paused at the intersection. *Good.* He didn't know which way to go. He must have heard me coming because he turned to look behind him and then darted into the passage on the right.

Perfect. It dead ended at the locked door that led to a building near Darling's salon. Danny and I had hidden the key to the lock at the intersection he'd just fled. When I reached the intersection, I reached up and retrieved the key from the top of a wooden beam above the doorway. I tucked it in my pocket as I ran. It wouldn't be long, and I'd round the corner and find the man waiting for me, with nowhere to run.

But before I did, he reemerged in the middle of the passageway.

He was holding a small blade.

I pulled up within eight feet of him. The metal door to the outside was locked right behind him. He was trapped.

"Why don't you let me call the police, and you can turn yourself in."

He made a disgusted sound.

"You're going to die down here." I said. "I mean, I'm not saying you don't deserve it. But it's really not a fair fight."

Before I finished speaking, he lunged at me with a metal pipe he'd been holding behind his back.

I managed to sidestep the blow in time for the pipe to glance off my shoulder instead of my skull. It still hurt like a son of a bitch though, and I cowered against the dirt wall for a few seconds to regain my bearings.

Before I could react, he lunged again. This time I grabbed hold of the end of the pipe but quickly let go when I realized it was jagged and had cut my palms.

Motherfucker.

This time he swung the pipe at my knees. I jumped back and avoided most of the impact but still felt the jagged end of the pipe slice open my jeans above the knee on one leg.

Then he was coming at me, the pipe above his head. I managed to plant a round kick to his ribs that sent him spinning. I regrouped to avoid his body and the swinging pipe and found myself backed against the metal door.

He'd backed up and was panting, holding the pipe out in front of him. Blood was still dripping from my hand.

He lifted the pipe above his head and took a step forward. As my back hit the door, I felt the Beretta in my waistband pressing into the small of my back under my shirt. I refused to admit that

I was trapped. I reached one hand behind me at the same time he gave a yell of exertion and came at me with the pipe.

There was nowhere to go. I managed to shift in time and the blow grazed my shoulder again, but still hard enough to send me crashing to my knees. I had the Beretta in my hand now.

He towered above me. The pipe was high above his head now. The muscles in his forearm were flexed. I could see that his eyes were glazed over with something—some kind of blood thirst. He looked inhuman.

At the last second, he shifted so he was sideways facing me. He gripped the pipe with his uninjured hand like it was a baseball bat and squared off. The pipe was at a right angle behind him, level with my eyes. He was going to tee off on my head.

The flash of metal as the pipe swung toward me was blurred out by the movement of me drawing my Beretta from behind me and firing off two shots in quick succession. The flash and boom echoed in the tunnel, and I was temporarily blinded and stunned.

Mid-swing, the pipe dropped from his hand and bounced off my leg.

He looked at me and laughed. Amped up as he was on adrenaline, he didn't yet know he'd been shot. Twice.

Even up close, I couldn't see where the bullets had entered. But I knew they had—I was too close to miss. For a second, listening to his laughter, I panicked. I watched as his eyes landed on the metal pipe. It had rolled closer to him. I started to reach for it. So did he. As he bent over, something happened.

The surprise had worn off. It sunk in. He'd been shot. I could see the realization flicker across his features as he slumped to his knees. His eyes rolled, and he toppled forward, landing on top of me.

I pushed him off in a frenzy, scrambling to get up and away

from his body and his blood and his lifeless eyes. I could barely breathe as I ran down the tunnel trying to get away from him.

At the fork in the tunnel, I stopped, bending over to put my hands on my knees. I was hyperventilating. When I finally caught my breath, I glanced behind me again. He hadn't moved. I cautiously walked back to check. He lay crumpled at an unnatural angle, his head splayed awkwardly to the side, one leg bent backward.

I leaned down carefully, keeping my eyes trained on his vacant stare and reached to feel for a pulse, already knowing what I would find.

52

He was dead.

My first instinct was to call the police. It would've been the natural response. But for the past two years, calling the police was like calling the devil. With the chief in charge I never knew who was going to answer and what kind of response to expect.

If I called 911 and reported I had killed a man in self-defense, there was a very good chance the chief would have me arrested for murder and possibly even manipulate evidence to make it stick.

It was so fucked up.

Then I turned back. I had to hide the body.

Back at the metal door, I grabbed the assassin by his boots and began to drag him back toward the intersection. As I neared, I saw a large figure standing where the four passages met. Danny.

"Gia?"

"It's me. Help me. I need to get rid of the body."

"Oh my God." Danny sounded like he was going to cry.

"You going to be okay helping me? I can probably do it on my own."

It was sort of a lie.

"You can?" he sounded relieved.

"Not really," I admitted. I was already out of breath from dragging the body as far as I had. Danny was trying not to look at the dead man at my feet. "I could actually use your help lifting him over the gate. We need to drop him into the sewer." There was about a foot high gap between the gate and the tunnel ceiling. I hoped we could make the body fit over it.

Whatever was in the sewer water below would hopefully get rid of any evidence we might have left on the body.

"Oh," Danny said.

It wasn't convincing, but he did reach down and grab the guy under the armpits. I noticed he wouldn't look at the man's face.

Twenty minutes later we were back at the intersection of the passageways, less one dead body.

"You going to be okay?" I asked Danny.

"Yeah."

"Go home and shower and then throw those clothes away."

"Okay."

He seemed a little out of it.

I reached out to touch his arm but then drew back. I didn't want to freak him out any more than he already was.

I watched his retreating back until I couldn't see him anymore, then I turned toward the other tunnel and headed to the basement of the building across the street from Darling's salon.

Kicking open the door, I stepped into the light as the sun rose above the hills to the East and began to fill city streets with a glowing golden light.

53

BLAKE LOOKED AROUND HIS ROOM ONE LAST TIME BEFORE CLOSING the door. He knew he wouldn't be returning. But he could only take his laptop bag and whatever fit inside. He didn't want to alert anyone that he was leaving town. Actually, he was leaving the country. He'd double-checked twice that he had his fake passport and that his boarding pass was saved to his phone. He'd get online at the café down the street and remotely erase everything on the server that had to do with Night Fall.

It was a last-minute safeguard measure he'd told nobody about. It also meant he'd have to go into hiding for life. By deleting the website entirely, he was effectively fucking over all the sellers and buyers who used the site. It would cost them billions of dollars. They'd be out for blood. But he had to do it to save his own neck.

If the FBI was ever able to connect him to Night Fall, he would go away for life. They might suspect, but they would need proof for it to hold up in court. They knew it was him. They knew Blake Crawford was the Night Fall founder and that he lived in San Francisco. But that was all they knew. Right then.

They didn't have proof that Ethan Anderson was Blake Crawford. And they couldn't connect him to Night Fall.

If they could, with that proof, he was screwed. He might even get the death penalty. That's what Carl had told him when they'd first started working together. Death was not off the table for federal kingpin convictions. Which was totally insane since even Charles Manson hadn't been sentenced to death.

He figured he had about twelve hours to flee the country. Anything longer than that, and he'd be fucked.

And he had less than an hour to destroy Night Fall completely. The chief had texted him saying the FBI and SWAT team was gathering at 8 a.m. and would hit his apartment at 9 a.m. The chief said he would be forced to turn over Blake's address at the 8 a.m. briefing.

He glanced at his watch. It was 5 a.m. He had plenty of time to escape unnoticed.

His roommate Kraig was still sleeping, so at least he didn't have to lie to him one last time. As he stepped out onto the porch, he surreptitiously glanced around with his peripheral vision to see if anyone was hanging out on his street who seemed suspicious. Not a single soul. Sometimes at this hour, there'd be someone waiting at the bus stop across the street, but this morning there was no one.

The café was four blocks down his street. He strode along. About two blocks down, he passed another bus stop. Here there were three people waiting for the bus. A woman in a skirt and heels carrying a briefcase, a guy with a stocking cap and baggie jeans, and an older man sitting with a cane and small shopping bag.

When he got to the block with the café, the sidewalks were filled with people. It was the beginning of a small business district with a gourmet market, boutique clothing stores, gift shops and restaurants, and his favorite café—Wilde.

He liked the spot because there was a small, cave-like back room where all the seats faced outward, so he could always have his back to the wall. And since most people wanted to be in the bustling front area with the huge windows, he could always find a seat back there.

After ordering his coffee and a mini bacon and gouda souf-flé, he shifted from foot to foot, waiting for his order. Behind his dark sunglasses, he kept watch on the other people in the café to see if anyone paid him any extra attention. Nobody did. He was paranoid. Of course, after Carl's warning he had good reason to be paranoid, but still.

He had been exceedingly careful in covering his tracks. He pushed down the memory of the holes he'd had to plug in Night Fall. Those were early mistakes made in the early days. If he developed the website today, none of those holes would be there. Live and learn.

A group of people came into the café, several talking. He glanced over. Wasn't that the guy from the bus stop with the stocking cap? Bearded, stocking-capped young men wearing flannel shirts were a dime a dozen in his neighborhood. They all were trying to look different and unique, and they all ended up looking exactly the same. This was just another cookie cutter guy trying to look like a hipster.

Armed with his soufflé and iced coffee, he entered the back room. Every seat was full. He began to panic. *Crap. Crap. Crap.* He glanced at his watch. He had to delete the website and catch his Uber in twenty minutes. He'd scheduled it to pick him up in front of the café.

A man in a dark blue shirt and slacks closed his laptop and bent to gather his belongings.

Perfect. As he waited for the man to vacate his seat, he surveyed the people on each side of the man. To the right sat a woman with dreadlocks. She was reading a beat-up paperback.

An Asian man in a silk shirt and designer sunglasses sat to the left, head bent over his phone, fingers tapping furiously.

Blake's entire body relaxed. All was good in the world. He still had plenty of time.

The man who had vacated the seat brushed by him slightly on his way out the narrow doorway. Blake bristled. But he soon was ensconced in his normal seat. The seat was still a little warm, which grossed him out, but soon he was immersed in the Night Fall world.

He was reluctant to destroy his baby. He'd been up all night grieving not only the death of his website but also the death of a dream.

He'd hoped to change the world. He'd hoped Night Fall would change society. He'd hoped that Night Fall would become his legacy.

He logged into the chat room one last time.

Carl had left several messages. The first one said, "Get the hell out of the country."

His pounding heart leapt up to his throat as he scrolled to the first message. "They've found you."

It would take one key stroke to encrypt his computer. He reached for the button. At the same time, the dreadlocked woman beside him jumped up screaming bloody murder. He turned his head in astonishment. When he turned his head back, his laptop was gone. It was in the hands of the stocking-capped punk he'd seen earlier.

The dreadlocked woman clasped one of his arms in an iron grip, and the Asian guy on the other side held his other.

"You are under arrest for conspiracy to commit murder, money laundering, computer hacking, and conspiracy to traffic narcotics," said a guy in a suit.

He watched as more than a half dozen people rose from the tables in the back room and headed his way. His mouth hung open in astonishment. Every single person in the cafe was in on it. They were all federal agents.

Amid the chaos, the stocking-capped man disappeared out the front door with his laptop in hand. That meant everything— every single damn thing on his laptop—would be accessible to the FBI. He couldn't be more fucked.

———

ONCE HE WAS SETTLED into the back of a nondescript FBI van, a female agent with a ponytail wearing aviator glasses and a bulletproof vest addressed him.

"I'm trained in Krav Maga, so I suggest you just kick back and relax while we speak and not try to escape or do anything foolish. Just so you know, this was a simultaneous operation. What that means is while we were here grabbing you, we also picked up your buddy, Carl, in Indiana. Because guess what we found when we were poking around? He's the one who stole a few million in bitcoin from you. He offered to turn state's witness against you before we even asked. He offered before we even had a chance to have a sit down like you and I are having."

Blake blinked. *What?* Everything was surreal. This couldn't be happening. *Carl* had stolen the bitcoin and not Charlie or that kid in the Tenderloin? Would Carl really turn on him that quickly?

"If I'm under arrest, why aren't I at the San Francisco jail?" Blake asked. The van was parked. Why wasn't he being transported to the police station? He had paid the police chief a heck of a lot of money to make sure no arrest would stick.

"Let's not get ahead of ourselves," she said. "We've got lots of time to talk about the chief. I expect the chief is getting ready for our briefing. Too bad we had it a few hours earlier."

54

I LIMPED INTO THE SALON, FAVORING MY INJURED LEG. I KNEW I looked like a fucking zombie.

I stumbled my way past two early bird stylists getting ready for their first appointments at six. I made my way toward the back room. One of the stylists gasped but then I heard someone else say, "It's just Gia."

"You know the Walking Dead Girl?"

"She's Darling's friend. You hush up."

By the time I got to the rear of the salon, the door to the back office was open. Darling rushed out holding a cup of coffee. "Good Lord. You okay, Gia?"

"Where's Rosie?" I asked.

Darling jutted her chin over to the corner. Rosalie was asleep, curled up on a velvet couch with a fur blanket over her. I'd left her with others too many late nights. Guilt swarmed over me.

"Gia?" Darling had been speaking. I turned to look at her so I could concentrate on what she was saying.

"You okay?" Darling said. "You're in really rough shape."

"You should see the other guy."

"He better be dead."

I nodded grimly.

She leaned over and frowned, looking at the cut on my temple.

"You're going to need stitches."

I shook my head. "Just send one of your stylists out for butterfly bandages."

"You sure?"

I nodded.

"Maybe you need to get checked out for a concussion?"

"I don't think so," I said. "But if I start feeling goofy, I promise I'll go to the doctor."

Her eyes narrowed. "You swear?"

"I do."

Finally, she smiled.

"You did it, honey," she said. She took my arm and led me to the couch. "Marcus just called me. The feds are heading for the police station now. They're assembling a SWAT team to take the chief down."

"Which station?"

"Substation. Here in the Tenderloin. The chief's car is parked out front. That's where the takedown is going to be."

"Gotta go."

I raced out before she could answer.

———

I MADE my way as quickly as I could, limping and hobbling in the direction of the police station. I caught a glimpse of myself in a mirrored storefront.

I *did* look like the walking dead. My hair was ratty, sticking up on one side, matted on the other. I had blood streaked down one side of my face.

The other side of my face was purple and blue as my new black eye emerged.

Where there wasn't blood on my face, there was dirt.

So cute.

As I grew near, I saw the parking lot was empty. But I could see figures moving in the morning shadows down the street. Heavy, armed, hulking figures. SWAT.

I stayed pressed against a recessed door so I wouldn't accidentally get shot. I watched, my heart pounding, as the SWAT team silently gestured and moved forward in a formation as graceful as a ballet troupe.

A woman with wide, frightened eyes rushed outside. Two men in SWAT suits quickly took her arms and raced away with her.

Then the SWAT members were at the station door. A bright light erupted and a thundering boom made me jump as they threw a flash bang grenade inside the door of the substation. There was shouting and then silence. Two men in bulletproof vests emblazoned with "FBI" on them raced to the front doors and waited out front. After a few seconds they went inside. I realized I was holding my breath as I waited.

Two news vans skidded to a stop across the street. TV reporters holding microphones, and cameramen carrying bulky equipment leaped out and raced toward the substation.

A man in an FBI-issued bulletproof vest stepped out to stop them, holding up his arm. They stopped and set up their cameras, craning their necks to see the substation front door. More reporters arrived, several with smaller digital cameras with telephoto lenses.

Finally, the doors opened and a few SWAT guys emerged, assault rifles pointed at the ground, shoulders relaxed. I was holding my breath. Any second now.

Then I saw him.

As he stepped out onto the front steps of the substation, the media erupted into a frenzy. Cameras clicked and whirred, and reporters shouted questions. As the chief was escorted closer, he blinked against the brightness of the camera flashes.

They were leading him toward a car near me.

As they neared, it almost seemed as if the FBI agents paused to let the media get a good picture of him. When they slowed, I stepped out of the doorway and into the bright light of a streetlamp. My movement caught the eye of one of the agents. When he looked over I smiled. He frowned, but there wasn't much he could do with both of his hands gripping the chief's arm.

Then the chief turned his head and our eyes met.

It seemed to last an eternity.

I broke eye contact first. But not before giving him the sweetest smile I could muster. Then I turned and walked away without a backward glance.

———

BACK IN DARLING'S SALON, we both sat on the loveseat and stared up at the TV, which was muted. "They're going to show it on the early morning news."

"I wouldn't mind seeing it again," I said.

"I guess the hackers relinquished the ransom on the city," Darling said, giving me a knowing look.

"Oh. Good to know."

Darling grabbed the remote and turned up the volume.

Her face crinkled into a frown.

"Where's James?" she said. "I know he'd want to see this. I thought he said he'd be back tonight."

I shook my head. I didn't want to explain that we'd had a fight, and he was at his mother's house, and that's why he'd dropped Rosalie off here. He must not have told Darling what was going on. He sure as hell never told *me* he'd be back tonight.

We stared at the TV as some stupid sitcom wrapped up. Then the news began.

"Here we go," Darling said.

Even though I'd just lived it, I still watched, wide-eyed, as the federal agents walked out of the San Francisco police station each holding an arm of the police chief. The news anchor said a crooked FBI agent had also been arrested and that the founder of the Night Fall website had also been taken down along with some of his associates.

My phone rang. I looked down at the number and wanted to cry in relief. It was James.

"Unbelievable," he said.

"Are you coming home now?"

He was quiet for a second. "Yes."

"I'll see you there."

55

DARLING HAD OFFERED TO KEEP ROSALIE FOR THE DAY.

I picked up some hot coffee and croissants on the way home. Even though I knew I looked a fright with an eye turning black and butterfly bandages across my temple, the cashier at the coffee shop didn't even give me a second glance. Sometimes living in San Francisco came in handy that way.

I was ecstatic when I walked into the loft.

I had big plans. We were going to celebrate the arrest of the chief with a good breakfast and really, really good sex.

But as soon as I walked in, I could tell James was in a major funk.

"You okay?" he said when he saw my face and leg, but it didn't seem like he was really that concerned. Not like Darling had been when she saw me. Then again, maybe he was more used to seeing me in such a state.

We ate our croissants in silence. It struck me as odd, but I figured James was in shock from everything that had happened. Even though it was ten in the morning, he got out a bottle of whiskey and drank a coffee mug full of it. I looked at him in surprise but didn't say anything. It wasn't up to me to judge how he reacted to the news that the man who'd put him in a wheel-chair was finally going to see justice served.

After breakfast, we headed to the bed. James was more rough and passionate than he'd ever been. I could get used to it. But after, as we lay there, I realized that something was off. Something big that I'd been trying to make excuses for all morning.

James was lying beside me staring at the ceiling. The tension was palpable.

"Hey, sailor," I said, reaching out to trial my fingers along his forearm. "I thought you'd be thrilled to hear the chief was finally getting what he deserved. What's going on?"

I also knew that sometimes when you'd waited so long for something, there couldn't help but be a small letdown when it finally happened.

He didn't answer. He just pulled himself to a sitting position. I sat up too. He had a look I'd never seen. I couldn't tell if he was furious or about to cry. He was working the inside of his lip with his teeth in a fury.

I was instantly alarmed. "James?"

Again, he didn't answer.

"James. Don't worry, the charges are going to stick. They've got him every which way from Sunday. They've got evidence to fill a small mansion. He's going away for life. There is no way he's going to squirm out of this one."

"It's not that."

"Then what?" I crawled out of bed and pulled on a robe. "Spill it."

"I don't know."

I was starting to get annoyed. I headed to the bathroom.

"Let me know when you figure it out," I said, throwing the words over my shoulder. All these weeks of him being crabby had finally taken their toll.

An extra-long shower didn't rid me of the foul mood I was in. What the fuck was wrong with him? I'd thought it was hopelessness over his hunt for the chief. I thought once the chief was put away, everything would be better.

I'd thought it was all about the chief. I was wrong. I was a fool.

Because when I came out of the shower, James was gone.

He hadn't even said goodbye.

————

I WAS on the rooftop staring into the distance wondering where it had all gone wrong when Django heard something and leapt to his feet, rushing for the door to the stairwell.

James was back.

I cautiously entered the loft, hoping I could gauge his mood.

He was pulling clothes off his low shelf in the closet and stuffing them into a duffel bag on his lap. I froze, my face growing ice cold.

When he heard me, he didn't even look up and kept his back to me as he said, "I'm going to Germany."

I stared at him. It seemed like all the oxygen had left the room. At the same time, all the moisture in my mouth had been sucked right out.

"Gia?"

"When do you leave?"

"My plane leaves in a few hours."

I nearly gasped.

"Mother is waiting downstairs to take me to the airport."

His words had shaken me, but his body language was even worse. He would barely look at me.

My perfect little domestic life had just imploded.

"What are you going to tell Rosalie?"

"I already did. I stopped by the salon first."

He told her before me. I knew on a deep level that this was bad. Very, very bad.

"And?" My mouth was dry. All moisture seemed to have been sucked out of it.

"She said that she would miss me, but she hoped I could walk again."

"That was it?"

He nodded.

Then, for the first time in the conversation, he met my eyes. "I'm sorry."

He put his duffel bag on his lap and wheeled himself into the elevator. I watched the doors slide closed as he looked down, not meeting my eyes.

56

MELISSA PAID FOR BLAKE'S ATTORNEY. SECRETLY. SHE TOLD HIM to never mention her name again. Not in public. Not in private. Never. And to never reach out in any shape or form whatsoever. As far as she was concerned, he was dead to her.

Blake understood. He knew that any connection between them would now mean political death for her. She'd be lucky if she could write off their college romance as a mistake that set the direction for her future. Maybe she could pitch it to sound like his desire to become a criminal inspired her to take up arms against crime. He wished he would've suggested this to her before she hung up on him. She'd been his one call.

He hadn't known where else to turn.

His parents would've wanted to help and hire an attorney, but Blake was facing federal charges that could lead to the death penalty. Melissa was the only person powerful and rich enough to find him an attorney who might save his life.

"I'll send you the best of the best, Ethan. Do exactly as he says," she told him. "If you don't, you're a fool who is wasting my money."

He winced. He'd never heard her so angry. But he took

comfort in knowing that one of the reasons she was so furious was because she still cared about him. If he was nobody to her, she not only wouldn't help, but she also wouldn't be so pissed off about it. That's why he'd decided to continue to go by the name Blake. Ethan was dead to him. Ethan was the man Melissa had once loved. That man was gone forever.

He waited for hours in the interview room for the attorney. Every once in a while, the guard would look in the small window, and Blake would give the thumbs up. The first time he'd done this, the guard had responded by flipping him off.

The attorney's name was Dolph Ballinger. Blake wondered if he'd be a big talker, full of promises to get Blake off.

At 3:00 p.m. the door opened and a man stepped inside. With his squat, muscular physique, longer hair, and square jaw, Dolph Ballinger looked more like an aging body builder than a high-powered attorney

He was not a man to mince words. Before Blake could stand to shake his hand, Dolph said, "Give them the police chief or you get the chair."

The attorney's ice-blue eyes cut right through him. Blake nodded slowly, somewhat in shock.

"Glad you're as smart as our mutual friend said." It wasn't lost on Blake that the attorney wouldn't speak Melissa's name aloud. "Do you want me to go over the charges against you? They are quite lengthy. Your former partner has made a plea deal. He's ready to turn over everything. He's already given up the ghost about you, Night Fall, the police chief. The hitman. Everything."

Carl had ended up being his worst enemy. He'd been stealing millions of dollars since the day Charlie left and blamed it on her. He'd lied about everything. He had been Blake's only friend. Only confidant. His consigliere. And he had screwed him over in the worst possible way. Any fight Ethan had left had seeped away when he released the enormity of Carl's betrayal.

"Are there any charges that won't stick?" he asked, listlessly.

"No," Dolph said.

"Then I don't care what the charges are," Blake said. He felt numb. None of this was real. He'd spent the night in a freezing cell curled up in the fetal position wondering when he'd wake from this nightmare. He realized now that the answer was never.

Dolph opened his briefcase and shuffled through some papers. "I'll make the arrangements for the plea deal, but I can't guarantee they'll take the death penalty off the table," he said, then stood and started toward the door. With one hand on the knob, he turned toward Blake.

"Any questions?"

"Will I die in prison?"

Blake closed his eyes, waiting for the answer.

"If you're lucky."

He didn't open his eyes again until he heard the door click closed.

57

Six weeks after James left me to go pursue the medical miracle that might allow him to walk again, I'd tried to get him back. I chased after him, telling him I'd move to Germany—that I'd follow him to Siberia if it meant staying together. I told him that Rosalie and I would do anything just to be near him again.

But it was too late.

Shortly after I'd arrived in Germany, he took me aside and told me he thought we needed a break, that he had to try out life without me. That we were too different and always would be.

Six fucking weeks apart, and he was done with me. It hurt so bad. I retreated back to San Francisco and curled up in the fetal position for a week before Darling came. She kicked the snot out of me verbally, telling me that I had to grow the fuck up and that I could no longer have the pity parties I used to indulge in because now I had a small child who relied on me.

Thank God for Darling.

I started working on getting healthy. I concentrated on my Budo and creating a safe, peaceful home life for Rosalie. I even started seeing a therapist. I was numb but not depressed. I just found myself feeling very sad at old songs I'd listened to with James or evenings when the sunset lit the sky up in a certain way. But I was okay. For once, I wasn't self-destructing when my life had fallen apart. Instead, I was picking up the pieces—slowly and one by one.

Seven months later, right when I thought I could possibly, just possibly, carve out a life without him, James called me.

I answered the phone because I saw it was an international number. My heart was racing in my throat but I sat there in stony silence until he spoke first.

"Gia, I don't want it to end this way," he said.

I waited a few beats, then said, "I guess you should've thought of that before."

"This separation was a long time coming."

That gave me pause. I thought back over the past year. I could honestly say I'd *never* seen it coming. Things had been tough, but I never thought we couldn't work through them.

"I'm going back into law enforcement. I spoke to the new police chief, and he said there would definitely be a spot for me when I come back in six months." He paused. "Whether I regain use of my legs or not."

"That's great James."

He was coming back. Did that mean he wanted to work it out with me?

"How's the treatment going?"

"Gia, it's a miracle," he said. For the first time in the conversation he didn't sound like he had a thousand-pound weight pressing down on him. "I could feel my toes the other day. I'm starting to get a tingling sensation in my thighs. I really think this could work."

I swallowed back my tears. I was so happy for him. The sheer joy in his voice was the best thing I'd ever heard.

"I was calling because..." again he paused. I held my breath. Did he want me back? Did he miss me that much? "See...I..." he trailed off.

"What?" My voice was soft, encouraging.

"There's no easy way to say it, so I'll just say it. I'm getting married."

I felt numb. He kept talking—something about falling in love with a nurse at the clinic and bringing her back to San Francisco, wanting me to know before I read it in the paper, his mother..."

It was all a white buzzing noise. The words "I'm getting married" kept echoing in my head.

"Gia? Gia?"

"Huh?"

"I'm really sorry. About everything."

"Me too." I hung up the phone with a gentle press of the pad of my finger. I didn't want to hear any more. I couldn't hear any more.

Rosalie was at school. I'd have to tell her when she got home. Then I realized I didn't have to tell her. She didn't understand the relationship anyway. She just knew James lived far away now. And she seemed okay with it.

Django looked at me and whined. I swear that dog could pick up on my moods.

I sat there in a daze. My first inclination was to unearth the massive bottle of bourbon on my topmost shelf, grab the pack of cigarettes I'd hidden in the front closet, and go drink and smoke until my pain went away. But then at the last minute I decided against it.

Darling's words echoed in my head. "Grow the fuck up, Gia."

Instead, I went up to the roof with Django trailing behind me. I sat and stared into the distance until my watch beeped that it was time to go get Rosalie from school.

I spent about a week in this same sort of detached daze. I didn't feel pain. I didn't feel happy. I felt numb.

58

BLAKE'S ATTORNEY WAS ALREADY IN THE SMALL WINDOWLESS ROOM when the guard led him in.

As soon as Blake stepped inside, Dolph Ballinger stood.

"I thought I should tell you this in person."

Blake immediately blanched. Was someone dead? Had having a criminal for a son finally given his father the heart attack they'd always worried about?

"All plea deals are off the table."

Blake sunk into a chair. His body limp with relief.

"What does that mean?"

"No pleas. No deals."

"I don't understand," Blake said, blinking.

"Your plea deal? No go. You'll face all charges," Dolph said. He reached for his briefcase and began walking toward the door. "Don't feel too bad because your buddy Carl's deal is off the table, as well."

"I don't understand."

"It's like this, son," Dolph said with his hand on the door-knob. "Apparently prosecutors received a massive file from some anonymous source that basically was a copy of everything your little website has ever done. There's enough evidence there to put all of you away for eternity."

Blake didn't even notice Dolph leave.

EPILOGUE

Six Months Later

As soon as the Mediterranean sun beating down on my bare skin became the slightest bit uncomfortable, a slight, cool, ocean breeze would sweep over me, making me sigh with something that felt like happiness. But I didn't trust it. I'd been wallowing in self pity for quite some time. I wasn't sure if I'd recognize happiness anymore.

I'd thrown a regular "pity party" as Darling would've called it. The man I loved had fallen out of love with me and was marrying someone else. Why did I think I was so special? This happened to people around the world every day.

Dante told me it just proved that someone better was out there for me.

But I didn't want someone better. I didn't want anyone. Ever again.

The sun was healing. I hadn't felt sad for two whole days. A record lately.

If I opened my eyes, all I saw was a stretch of white sand leading to a turquoise sea that went on for miles. The only sound was the gentle lapping of waves on the beach. And the occasional slight rustling of Dante turning the pages of his paperback.

The silence was broken by the loud grumbling of my stomach.

Dante laughed. It was a good sound to hear.

"Oh my," Dante suddenly said in a tone that made me sit up, squinting.

Out of the sea came a beautiful man. A blonde Poseidon emerging from the water onto our deserted stretch of beach, water dripping off of him. Beyond him, I saw a small boat bobbing in the waves a little bit out.

"Jesus Christ," I said as the man got closer, and I saw white teeth against bronzed skin as he smiled. He was quite the specimen.

It was the first time my best friend and I had both been single at the same time. I'd let him talk me into this vacation to St. Tropez. Rosalie was staying with Darling for the week. At first, I'd been worried about leaving her but reassured myself that she was in good hands.

It had been a whirlwind trip so far, visiting a bunch of Dante's mega-rich friends, eating at all the best restaurants, but mostly lying on the beach all day not doing a damn thing. Dante had tried to set me up on dates or even one-night stands with several of the good-looking young men who ran in the Riviera crowd, and even some of the older, sophisticated men who owned yachts and villas. But I wasn't interested.

Dante and I had gone out to dinner the night before.

The restaurant patio was candlelit, and in the distance we could hear the crashing waves as we spoke of the men we had loved and lost.

Years ago, we'd both had our greatest loves snatched from us by a murderer. Dante had lost his husband, Matt, and I'd lost my boyfriend, Bobby.

Since then, Dante had had a few boyfriends, but nobody serious.

I'd had James.

Now we were alone again.

I wanted to feel sorry for myself, but Dante was so damn smiling and happy.

"What?" I said, taking another sip of my wine.

His face glowed in the candlelight illuminating his dark Italian skin and white teeth that had made me fall in love with him as a teenage girl—until he'd confessed he preferred boys.

"Gia, don't be sad."

"I'm trying. I'm really trying."

"Love never dies."

"That sounds like so trite, like a greeting card."

"But it's true. Love leaves enduring traces that continue to guide us and influence us for the rest of our lives. It's not a physical or tangible thing. It can't die."

I made a face but then really thought about what he said.

I shrugged. "I don't know. Why does it hurt so badly then?"

"It's how you look at it," he said, reaching over and placing his hand on mine. "You can relive the memories with pleasure or with pain. It's up to you."

The painful part was the realization that maybe James was right when we'd first met and he said trying to make it work was hopeless—he was a cop through and through, and I was a lawbreaker through and through. Maybe we had never had a chance after all. But that didn't mean I didn't love that man—I did love him.

It was so freeing to say it. *I loved him.* He was not mine, but I loved him. I wished him the best in life. I wished him the happiness he deserved. That must be what true love was—to love someone so much that you wanted their happiness even if meant they were happy without you.

Now, on the beach, I lifted my faced to the sun, closing my eyes and breathing deeply, grateful to be alive. I was grateful to feel what love was.

I would be okay. I always was. I'd been so full of hate when I'd first been orphaned that I'd ended up hating myself. I'd been so full of hate when Bobby had been murdered, I'd been unable to love again for a long time.

James had showed me that I could love. And by loving me and leaving me, he'd shown that I was stronger than I thought. That I could love somebody from afar even if they didn't feel the same sort of love for me. That love never truly died.

I also had gotten real with myself. Dante was right. Love was not tangible. It wasn't something you could hold tight to.

Loving someone meant setting them free. I had not done that. I'd clipped James's wings. I had tried to stop him from going to Germany. I had clung too tightly. It was a huge mistake that had cost me big time. It had cost me *him*.

The brilliant sun beating down on my body filled me with an unexpected calm and peace. As long as I could feel the way I felt right now, I would be okay.

As long as I continued to love more than hate, I would survive.

We both watched the man grow closer. He looked like a Dolce & Gabbana model paid to seduce us. Sun-bleached hair, sculpted, tanned body, brilliant white smile.

Maybe a few kisses. This guy definitely had a body worth kissing.

And then he spoke with a husky, deep voice. "*Bon jour.*"

"*Enchanté,*" Dante said, already laying on the charm.

I kept my eyes on the man coming closer.

"I got dibs," Dante said to me in a whisper.

I lifted my sunglasses and smiled at the man as I said under my breath, "We'll see about that."

The story continues in *Stone Cold*, the next Gia Santella Thriller. Head to the next page for a sneak peek or scan the QR code below to order today!

Stay up to date with Kristi Belcamino's new releases by scanning the QR code below!
(You'll receive a **free** copy of *First Vengeance: A Gia Santella Prequel!*)

Did you enjoy *Night Fall*? Scan the QR code below to let us know your thoughts!

STONE COLD CHAPTER ONE

Rosalie shuffled the playing cards, expertly executing a one-handed shuffle that would make any Vegas dealer proud. She then dealt the cards with precision, each card lying perfectly on top of the one thrown before it.

Dante waited until all of his cards were before him on the black oak table before he scooped them up and gave me a look, raising his eyebrow.

"What?" I said.

"You guys play poker a lot?"

"Maybe. Got a problem with that?"

"I'm not sure it's appropriate for a nine-year-old to be a card shark, that's all."

"Oh, don't be such an old man," I said. "Besides, it's card sharp."

"Sharp?"

"Sharp."

"It's not shark?"

"Nope," I said.

"That's dumb." He rolled his eyes.

Rosalie laughed. It was wonderful to see her so lighthearted.

This was a far cry from the kid who'd crawled into the back of my Jeep two years ago with ICE agents chasing after her.

She'd seen loved ones raped and murdered, witnessing worse violence than most hard-core gang members serving in San Quentin.

"After this game, can we show Dante our card trick?" she asked, not taking her gaze off the cards she held splayed in her hand.

"Most definitely," I said.

My friend, Danny, the best hacker in San Francisco, had taught her a crazy cool card trick. She loved showing it off.

Later, after Rosalie had taken all our quarters at poker and shown Dante her card trick, I'd sent her to bed with Django, the Pitbull-mix dog who used to be mine.

Once I heard both Rosalie and the dog snoring in her bedroom, Dante and I headed to the rooftop of the loft.

It was summer in San Francisco—which meant, of course, that it was freezing—so I lit both heat lamps, and we wrapped ourselves in thick blankets as we sprawled in the lounge chairs under my grape arbor.

In the distance, to the east, I could see the glow of the Bay Bridge beyond the downtown skyscrapers dotted with white lights.

The sky to the west looked turbulent, a roiling gray and black mass.

"Storm's coming in," Dante said, looking the same way.

"Glad you're staying over."

Dante lived in Calistoga but was down in the city for a board meeting for my company, Ethel's Place.

Ethel's Place, named after my friend who was murdered, helped homeless people who wanted to get back into society. We built multi-use buildings that offered apartments upstairs and retail shops on the street level where the residents could work and train for up to a year—getting them off the streets, employing them, and giving them skills to set out on their own later on.

After getting the business up and running, I was basically a figurehead on the board but still tried to attend quarterly meetings.

I knew Dante always felt torn leaving his restaurants, but I was selfish and wanted his company, so I begged him to come down for the meeting early and stay the night.

We'd taken Rosalie to dinner at some hip, up-and-coming restaurant Dante had wanted to do recon on. "Not bad," had been his verdict after we'd shelled out three hundred bucks for three tiny meals of unidentifiable foods. I'd had to drive through Mickey D's after so Rosalie would actually have some food in her before bed.

Huddled under blankets on my roof, I reached over to a small, jeweled box I'd hidden in the palm plant and extracted a small joint. I puffed on it a few times and passed it to Dante.

"Rosalie's a great kid," he said.

I beamed in the dark. "I know, right?"

"Does she ever talk about James?"

"Sure," I said. "She goes over there sometimes."

"She does?"

"Yeah. Well, every Thursday. Why do you act so surprised?"

James was my ex-boyfriend. When Rosalie had first come into my life, I'd been with James, and for a while, we'd been a family.

Until he dumped me.

I grabbed the joint from Dante and inhaled. Only after I exhaled did I speak.

"He just had a kid."

It was the first time I'd said the words out loud, and it hurt less than I'd thought it would.

"Really?" Dante said.

When James had been shot and paralyzed by his own colleagues on the San Francisco Police Department, the doctors had questioned whether he'd ever be able to have children or even walk again. He'd undergone some experimental stem cell treatment overseas after we'd broken up, and, though he still used a wheelchair, he was regaining feeling and limited use of his legs. While his manhood had still been, uh, very, very functional after the accident, his baby-making ability had been in doubt. Until now, I guess.

"Good for him."

"Yeah." I was quiet.

"You okay with all that?"

"I guess." I stubbed out the joint.

"Gia?"

"I still love him. I want him to be happy. That's what real grown up love is, right?"

Dante gave a bitter laugh. "Yeah."

"Well, it sucks."

We both burst out laughing.

One fateful night a few years back, we'd both lost everything to murderers. Dante lost his husband of only a few hours, Matt. I'd lost my boyfriend, Bobby.

Now, we both sat in silence. We'd been best friends for so long that it didn't take words for me to know we were both remembering that horrific night.

"I guess I'm destined to be alone forever," I said.

Dante surprised me by jumping up and slipping under the blanket with me on my chaise lounge. He laid his head on my shoulder and whispered. "Silly, Gia. You have me. You'll never be alone. Not as long as I walk this earth."

Leaning down, I kissed his brow.

He was right.

I was the luckiest girl in the world.

"Do you think Rosalie will grow up and take care of us when we're old?" I said.

"Uh, yeah. Duh," he said. "We're going to be two doddering old fools drinking our whiskey sours, and she's going to be our boss, scolding us not to drink and smoke weed. And we'll just cackle with laughter."

I got caught up in the fantasy.

"Can we live on the beach?"

"Yes!"

"And Rosalie will have kids, so in a way we'll be like grand-parents, right?"

"Of course!" Dante said. "We'll be the coolest grandparents ever. We'll tell them stories about how naughty we were when we were their age!"

"Oh, we better not!" I said.

"Oh, we *will*!"

I closed my eyes, imagining a life many years down the road when I was a gray-haired grandma in a rocking chair at a beach house watching children play in the waves in front of me and sipping my cocktail as the sun set.

My reverie was interrupted by a loud alarm on my phone.

Somebody was at the front door downstairs. I jumped up in surprise.

Nobody should have been able to get that far inside my building without other alarms going off.

I quickly grabbed the phone and clicked to the camera outside my steel front door. It was an older woman whom I didn't recognize. How in the hell had she gotten into the building?

I was up and down the stairs with Dante at my heels.

Once down in the loft, I reached up into my closet and extracted my Glock from the gun safe before I ordered Dante into Rosalie's bedroom. "Go in and lock that door until I call for you."

He didn't argue.

STONE COLD CHAPTER TWO

It had all unfurled according to his plans.

It was nearly over.

Patience and persistence had gotten him this far.

It would serve him to the end.

And then he would be free.

Only a few more pieces of the puzzle and everything would fall into place.

His loyalty, his tenacity, his superior intelligence, would all be recognized and rewarded.

Soon.

For now, though, it was business as usual.

Are you loving *Stone Cold*? Scan the QR code below to order your copy today!

ALSO BY KRISTI BELCAMINO

Enjoying Kristi Belcamino? Scan the code below to see her Amazon Author page!

Gia Santella Crime Thriller Series

Vendetta

Vigilante

Vengeance

Black Widow

Day of the Dead

Border Line

Night Fall

Stone Cold

Cold as Death

Cold Blooded

Dark Shadows

Dark Vengeance

Dark Justice

Deadly Justice

Deadly Lies

Additional books in series:

Taste of Vengeance

Lone Raven

Vigilante Crime Series

Blood & Roses

Blood & Fire

Blood & Bone

Blood & Tears

Queen of Spades Thrillers

Queen of Spades

The One-Eyed Jack

The Suicide King

The Ace of Clubs

The Joker

The Wild Card

High Stakes

Poker Face

Standalone Novels

Coming For You

Sanctuary City

The Girl in the River

Buried Secrets

Dead Wrong (Young Adult Mystery)

Gabriella Giovanni Mystery Series

Blessed are the Dead

Blessed are the Meek

Blessed are Those Who Weep

Blessed are Those Who Mourn

Blessed are the Peacemakers

Blessed are the Merciful

Nonfiction

Letters from a Serial Killer

ALSO BY WITHOUT WARRANT

More Thriller Series from Without Warrant Authors

Dana Gray Mysteries by C.J. Cross

Girl Left Behind

Girl on the Hill

Girl in the Grave

The Kenzie Gilmore Series by Biba Pearce

Afterburn

Dead Heat

Heatwave

Burnout

Deep Heat

Fever Pitch

Storm Surge (Coming Soon)

Willow Grace FBI Thrillers by Anya Mora

Shadow of Grace

Condition of Grace (Coming Soon)

Gia Santella Crime Thriller Series

by Kristi Belcamino

Vendetta

Vigilante

Vengeance

Black Widow

Day of the Dead

Border Line

Night Fall

Stone Cold

Cold as Death

Cold Blooded

Dark Shadows

Dark Vengeance

Dark Justice

Deadly Justice

Deadly Lies

Vigilante Crime Series by Kristi Belcamino

Blood & Roses

Blood & Fire

Blood & Bone

Blood & Tears

Queen of Spades Thrillers by Kristi Belcamino

Queen of Spades

The One-Eyed Jack

The Suicide King

The Ace of Clubs

The Joker

The Wild Card

High Stakes

Poker Face

AUTHOR'S NOTE

When I was 16, I read Jackie Collins' book, *Lucky*, and it rocked my world. For the first time in my prolific reading life (yes, I was the kid holed up in my room reading as many books as I could as often as I could), I met a character who was not only Italian-American like me, but a strong, powerful, and successful badass woman who didn't take crap from anybody and loved to have sex!

Although I had dreamed of being a writer, it never seemed like a realistic dream and my attempts at writing seemed pitiful. So I studied journalism and became a reporter—it was a way to be a writer and have a steady paycheck.

It was only when I was in my forties that I got the guts to write a book. And it was a few years after that I was brave enough to write the character I really wanted to write—Gia Santella.

She's not Lucky Santangelo, of course. I mean, nobody could be as cool as Lucky is, but I like to think that maybe Gia and Lucky would have been friends.

Gia is my alter ego. The woman who does and says things I

never could or would, but whom I admire and would love to be friends with.

If you like her, I'm pretty sure we'd be the best of friends in real life!

x Kristi

ABOUT THE AUTHOR

Kristi Belcamino is a USA Today bestseller, an Agatha, Anthony, Barry & Macavity finalist, and an Italian Mama who bakes a tasty biscotti.

Her books feature strong, kickass, independent women facing unspeakable evil in order to seek justice for those unable to do so themselves.

In her former life, as an award-winning crime reporter at newspapers in California, she flew over Big Sur in an FA-18 jet with the Blue Angels, raced a Dodge Viper at Laguna Seca, attended barbecues at the morgue, and conversed with serial killers.

During her decade covering crime, Belcamino wrote and reported about many high-profile cases including the Laci Peterson murder and Chandra Levy disappearance. She has appeared on *Inside Edition* and local television shows. She now writes fiction and works part-time as a reporter covering the police beat for the St. Paul *Pioneer Press*.

Her work has appeared in such prominent publications as *Salon*, the *Miami Herald*, *San Jose Mercury News,* and *Chicago Tribune*.

facebook.com/kristibelcaminowriter
instagram.com/kristibelcaminobooks
tiktok.com/@kristibelcaminobooks

Printed in the USA
CPSIA information can be obtained
at www.ICGtesting.com
LVHW010331050224
770948LV00027B/675